SLAY-RIDE

Dick Francis has written forty-one international bestsellers and is widely acclaimed as one of the world's finest thriller writers. His awards include the Crime Writers' Association's Cartier Diamond Dagger for his outstanding contribution to the crime genre, and an honorary Doctorate of Humane Letters from Tufts University of Boston. In 1996 Dick Francis was made a Mystery Writers of America Grand Master for a lifetime's achievement and in 2000 he received a CBE in the Queen's Birthday Honours list.

Dick Francis

SLAY-RIDE

PAN BOOKS

First published 1973 by Michael Joseph Ltd

This edition published 1974 by Pan Books
an imprint of Pan Macmillan, a division of Macmillan Publishers Limited
Pan Macmillan, 20 New Wharf Road, London N1 9RR
Basingstoke and Oxford
Associated companies throughout the world
www.panmacmillan.com

ISBN 978-0-330-51919-9

1 3 5 7 9 8 6 4 2

A CIP catalogue record for this book is available from
the British Library.

Phototypeset by Intype London Ltd
Printed and bound in the UK by
CPI Mackays, Chatham ME5 8TD

CHAPTER ONE

Cold grey water lapped the flimsy-looking sides of the fibre-glass dinghy, and I shivered and thought of the five hundred feet straight down to the sea-bed underneath.

An hour out of Oslo with the outboard motor stilled and my friend Arne Kristiansen taking all afternoon to answer some simple questions.

A grey day, damp, not far from rain. The air sang in my ears with stinging chill. My feet were congealing. The October temperature down the fjord was giving the land a twenty degree lead towards zero, and of the two of us only Arne was dressed for it.

Where I had a showerproof jacket over an ordinary suit and no hat, he had come equipped with the full bit: a red padded cap with ear flaps fastened with a strap under his chin, blue padded trousers tucked into short wide-legged gumboots, and a red padded jacket fastened up the front with silver coloured press studs. A glimpse of black and yellow at the neck spoke of other warm layers underneath.

He had arranged on the telephone to meet me at

1

the statue in the Radhusplassen by the harbour, brushing aside my suggestion that he should come to the Grand Hotel, where I was staying. Even in those wide open spaces he had gone muttering on about being overheard by long range bugging machines (his words) and had finally insisted on taking to the dinghy. Knowing from past experience the quickest way in the end to deal with his perennial mild persecution complex was to go along with it, I had shrugged and followed him along the quay to where the small pale green craft bobbed beside a flight of steps.

I had forgotten that it is always very much colder out on open water. I flexed the stiffening fingers inside my pockets and repeated my last question.

'How would you smuggle sixteen thousand stolen kroner out of the country?'

For the second time, I got no answer. Arne produced answers as prodigally as tax collectors offer rebates.

He blinked slowly, the dropping of the eyelids marking some intermediary stage in the chess-like per-mutations going on in his head. He was no doubt, as always, considering every foreseeable consequence: if answer A might produce any one of five responses, and answer B lead on to six subsidiary questions, wouldn't it be wiser to answer C, in which case, though . . .

It made conversation with him a trifle slow.

I tried a little prompting. 'You said it was all in coins

and used notes of small denominations. How bulky? Enough to fit in a small sized suitcase?'

He blinked.

'Do you think he just walked out with it through the customs?'

He blinked.

'Or do you think he is still somewhere in Norway?'

Arne opened his mouth and said grudgingly, 'No one knows.'

I tried some more. 'When a foreigner stays in one of your hotels, he has to fill in a form and show his passport. These forms are for the police. Have your police checked those forms?'

Pause.

'Yes,' he said.

'And?'

'Robert Sherman did not fill in any form.'

'None at all? What about when he arrived from England?'

'He did not stay in an hotel.'

Patience, I thought. Give me patience.

'Where, then?'

'With friends.'

'What friends?'

He considered. I knew he knew the answer. He knew he was eventually going to tell me. I suppose he couldn't help the way his mind worked, but this, God help us, was supposed to be an investigator.

What was more, I had taught him myself. 'Think

before you answer any question,' I'd said. So now he
did.

In the three months he had spent in England
learning how the Jockey Club ran its investigation
department we had grown to know each other well.
Some of the time he had stayed in my flat, most of the
time we had travelled together to the races, all of
the time he had asked and listened and blinked as he
thought. That had been three years ago. Two minutes
had been enough to resuscitate the old warm feelings
of tolerant regard. I liked him, I thought, more
because of the mild eccentric kinks than despite.

'He stayed with Gunnar Holth,' he said.

I waited.

After ten seconds he added, 'He is a racehorse
trainer.'

'Did Bob Sherman ride for him?'

This dead simple question threw him into a longer
than ever session of mental chess, but finally he said,
'Bob Sherman rode the ones of his horses which ran
in hurdle races while Bob Sherman was in Norway. *Ja*.
He did not ride the horses of Gunnar Holth which ran
in flat races while he was in Norway.'

God give me strength.

Arne hadn't actually finished. 'Robert Sherman rode
horses for the racecourse.'

I was puzzled. 'How do you mean?'

He consulted his inner man again, who evidently
said it was OK to explain.

'The racecourse pays appearance money to some foreign jockeys, to get them to come to Norway. It makes the racing more interesting for the racegoers. So the racecourse paid Robert Sherman to ride.'

'How much did they pay him?'

A rising breeze was stirring the fjord's surface into proper little wavelets. The fjord just below Oslo is not one of those narrow canyon jobs on the Come-To-Scenic-Norway posters, but a wide expanse of sea dotted with rocky islands and fringed by the sprawling suburbs of the city. A coastal steamer surged past half a mile away and tossed us lightly in its wake. The nearest land looked a lot further off.

'Let's go back,' I said abruptly.

'No, no . . .' He had no patience for such weak suggestions. 'They paid him fifteen hundred kroner.'

'I'm cold,' I said.

He looked surprised. 'It is not winter yet.'

I made a noise which was half laugh and half teeth beginning to chatter. 'It isn't summer either.'

He looked vaguely all around. 'Robert Sherman had made six visits to race in Norway,' he said. 'This was his seventh.'

'Look, Arne, tell me about it back at the hotel, huh?'

He attended to me seriously. 'What is the matter?'

'I don't like heights,' I said.

He looked blank. I took one frozen mitt out of its pocket, hung it over the side of the boat, and pointed straight down. Arne's face melted into comprehension and a huge grin took the place of the usual tight careful configuration of his mouth.

'David, I am sorry. The water to me, it is home. Like snow. I am sorry.'

He turned at once to start the outboard, and then paused to say, 'He could simply have driven over the border to Sweden. The customs, they would not search for kroner.'

'In what car?' I asked.

He thought it over. 'Ah yes.' He blinked a bit. 'Perhaps a friend drove him . . .'

'Start the engine,' I said encouragingly.

He shrugged and gave several small nods of the head, but turned to the outboard and pressed the necessary knobs. I had half expected it to prove as lifeless as my fingers, but the spark hit the gas in an orderly fashion and Arne pointed the sharp end back towards hot coffee and radiators.

The dinghy slapped busily through the little waves and the crosswind flicked spray on to my left cheek. I pulled my jacket collar up and made like a tortoise.

Arne's mouth moved as he said something, but against the combined noises of the engine and the sea and the rustle of gaberdine against my ears, I couldn't hear any words.

'What?' I shouted.

He started to repeat whatever it was, but louder. I caught only snatches like 'ungrateful pig' and 'dirty thief', which I took to be his own private views of

6

Robert Sherman, British steeplechase jockey. Arne had had a bad time since the said Bob Sherman disappeared with the day's take from the turnstiles of Øvrevoll, because Arne Kristiansen, besides being the Norwegian Jockey Club's official investigator, was also in charge of racecourse security.

The theft, he had told me on the outward chug, was an insult, first to himself, and secondly to Norway. Guests in a foreign country should not steal. Norwegians were not criminals, he said, and quoted jail statistics per million of population to prove it. When the British were in Norway, they should keep their hands to themselves.

Commiserating, I refrained from drawing his country's raids on Britain to his attention: they were, after all, a thousand or so years in the past, and the modern Vikings were less likely to burn, rape, pillage and plunder than to take peaceable photographs of Buckingham Palace. I felt moreover a twinge of national shame about Bob Sherman: I had found myself apologizing, of all things, for his behaviour.

Arne was still going on about it: on that subject unfortunately he needed no prompting. Phrases like 'put me in an intolerable position' slid off his tongue as if he had been practising them for weeks – which, on reflection, of course he had. It was three weeks and four days since the theft: and forty-eight hours since the Chairman of the racecourse had telephoned and asked me to send over a British Jockey Club investigator to see what he could do. I had sent (you will have guessed) myself.

I hadn't met the Chairman yet, nor seen the race-course, nor ever before been to Norway. I was down the fjord with Arne because Arne was the devil I knew.

Three years earlier the hair now closely hidden under the red padded hood had been a bright blond fading at the temples to grey. The eyes were as fierce a blue as ever, the wrinkles around them as deep, and the bags below a good deal heavier. The spray blew on to skin that was weather-beaten but not sunburned; thick-looking impervious yellowish-white skin lumped and pitted by forty-something winters.

He was still breaking out in bursts of aggrieved half-heard monologue, trudging along well-worn paths of resentment. I gave up trying to listen. It was too cold.

He stopped in mid-sentence and looked with raised eyebrows at some distant point over my left shoulder. I turned. A large speedboat, not very far away, was slicing down the fjord in our general direction with its bow waves leaping out like heavy silver wings.

I turned back to Arne. He shrugged and looked uninterested, and the outboard chose that moment to splutter and cough and choke to silence.

'*Fanden*,' said Arne loudly, which was nothing at all to what I was saying in my head.

'Those people will help us,' he announced, pointing at the approaching speedboat, and without hesitation he stood up, braced his legs, and waved his scarlet clad arms in wide sweeps above his head.

Twisting on my bench seat, I watched the speedboat draw near.

'They will take us on board,' Arne said.

The speedboat did not seem to be slowing down. I could see its shining black hull and its sharp cutting bow, and the silver wings of wave looked as high and full as ever.

If not higher and fuller.

I turned to Arne with the beginnings of apprehension.

'They haven't seen us,' I said.

'They must have.' Arne waved his arms with urgent acceleration, rocking the dinghy precariously.

'Hey!' Arne shouted to the speedboat. And after that he screamed at it, in Norwegian.

The wind blew his words away. The helmsman of the speedboat didn't hear, didn't see. The sharp hard shining black prow raced straight towards us at forty knots.

'Jump!' yelled Arne; and he jumped. A flash of scarlet streaking into the sea.

I was slow. Thought perhaps that the unimaginable wouldn't happen, that the bow wave would toss the dinghy clear like it would a swan, that the frail craft would bob away as lightly as a bird.

I tumbled over the side into the water about one second before the bow split the fibre-glass open like an eggshell. Something hit me a colossal bang on the shoulder while I was still gasping from the shock of immersion and I went down under the surface into a roaring buffeting darkness.

People who fall off boats die as often from the propellers as from drowning, but I didn't remember that until the twin screws had churned past and left me unsliced. I came stuttering and gulping to the daylight in the jumbled frothing wake and saw the back of the speedboat tearing away unconcernedly down the fjord.

'Arne,' I shouted, which was about as useless as dredging for diamonds in the Thames. A wave slapped me in the open mouth and I swallowed a double salt water, neat.

The sea seemed much rougher at face level than it had done from above. I floundered in high choppy waves with ruffles of white frothing across their tops and blowing into my eyes, and I shouted again for Arne. Shouted with intensifying concern for him and with fear for myself: but the wind tore the words away and battered them to bits.

There was no sign of the dinghy. My last impression was that it had been cut clean into two pieces, which were now, no doubt, turning over and over in a slow sink down to the far away sea-bed.

I shuddered as much from imagination as from cold.

There was no sight anywhere of Arne. No red-padded head, no red waving arms above the waves, no cheerful smile coming to tell me that the sea was home to him and that safety and hot muffins were *this* way, just over here.

Land lay visible all around me in greyish misty heights. None of it was especially near. About two miles away, I guessed, whichever way I looked.

Treading water, I began to pull my clothes off, still looking desperately for Arne, still expecting to see him.

There was nothing but the rough slapping water. I thought about the speedboat's propellers and I thought about Arne's wide legged gumboots which would fill with water in the first few seconds. I thought finally that if I didn't accept that Arne was gone and get started shorewards I was very likely going to drown on that spot.

I kicked off my shoes and struggled with the zip of my raincoat. Ripped open the buttons of my suit jacket underneath and shrugged out of both coats together. I let go of them, then remembered my wallet, and although it seemed crazy I took it out of my jacket pocket and shoved it inside my shirt.

The two coats, waterlogged, floated briefly away and started to go down out of sight. I slid out of my trousers, and let them follow.

Pity, I thought. Nice suit, that had been.

The water was very cold indeed.

I began to swim. Up the fjord. Towards Oslo. Where else?

*

I was thirty-three and hardy and I knew more statistics than I cared to. I knew for instance that the average human can live less than an hour in water of one degree centigrade.

I tried to swim unhurriedly in long undemanding strokes, postponing the moment of exhaustion. The water in Oslo fjord was not one degree above freezing, but at least five. Probably not much colder than the stuff buffeting the English beach at Brighton at that very moment. In water five degrees above freezing, one could last . . . well, I didn't actually know *that* statistic. Had to take it on trust. Long enough anyway to swim something over two miles.

Bits of distant geography lessons made no sense. 'The Gulf Stream warms the coast of Norway . . .' Good old Gulf Stream. Where had it gone?

Cold had never seemed a positive force to me before. I supposed I had never really been *cold*, just chilled. This cold dug deep into every muscle and ached in my gut. Feeling had gone from my hands and feet, and my arms and legs felt heavy. The best long-distance swimmers had a nice thick insulating layer of subcutaneous fat: I hadn't. They also covered themselves with water-repelling grease and swam alongside comfort boats which fed them hot cocoa through tubes on demand. The best long-distance swimmers were, of course, usually going twenty miles or so further than I was.

I swam.

The waves seemed frighteningly big: and I couldn't see where I was aiming unless I lifted my head right up and trod water, and that wasted time and energy.

The nearest-looking land seemed to my salt-stinging eyes to be as far away as ever. And surely Oslo fjord should be a Piccadilly Circus of boats? But I couldn't see a single one.

Dammit, I thought. I'm bloody well not going to drown. I'm bloody well *not*.

I swam.

Daylight was slowly fading. Sea, sky, and distant mountains were all a darker grey. It began to rain.

I travelled, it seemed, very slowly. The land I was aiming for never appeared to be nearer. I began to wonder if some current was cancelling out every yard I swam forward: but when I looked back, the land behind was definitely receding.

I swam mechanically, growing tired.

Time passed.

A long way off, straight ahead, pinpricks of light sprang out against the fading afternoon. Every time I looked, there were more. The city was switching on in the dusk.

Too far, I thought. They are too far for me. Land and life all around me, and I couldn't reach them.

An awful depth beneath. And I never did like heights. A cold lonely death, drowning.

I swam. Nothing else to do.

When another light shone out higher up and to the left, it took at least a minute for the news to reach my sluggish brain. I trod water and wiped the rain and sea out of my eyes as best I could and tried to make out where it came from: and there, a great deal nearer than when I'd last looked, was the solid grey shape of land.

Houses, lights, and people. All there, somewhere, on that rocky hump.

Gratefully I veered fifteen degrees left and pressed on faster, pouring out the carefully hoarded reserves of stamina like a penitent miser. And that was stupid, because no shelving beach lay ahead. The precious land, when I reached it, proved to be a smooth sheer cliff dropping perpendicularly into the water. Not a ledge, not a cranny, to offer even respite from the effort of staying afloat.

The last quarter mile was the worst. I could *touch* the land if I wanted to, and it offered nothing to cling to. There had to be a break somewhere, if I went far enough, but I had practically nothing left. I struggled feebly forward through the slapping waves, wishing in a hazy way that I could surge through warm calm water like Mark Spitz and make a positive touchdown against a nice firm rail, with my feet on the bottom. What I actually did was a sort of belly-flop on to a small boat slipway bordered with large rock slabs.

I lay half in and half out of the water, trying to get

back breath I didn't know I'd lost. My chest heaved. I coughed.

It wasn't dark; just the slow northern twilight. I wouldn't have minded if it had been three in the morning: the cold wet concrete beneath my cheek felt as warm and welcoming goose feathers.

Footsteps crunched rhythmically along the quay at the head of the slipway and then suddenly stopped.

I did a bit towards lifting my head and flapping a numb hand.

'*Hvem er der?*' he said; or something like it.

I gave a sort of croak and he walked carefully, crabwise, down the slipway towards me, a half seen, well-wrapped figure in the rainy gloom.

He repeated his question, which I still didn't understand.

'I'm English,' I said. 'Can you help me?'

Nothing happened for a few seconds. Then he went away.

So what, I thought tiredly. At least from the waist up I was safe in Norway. Didn't seem to have the energy to drag myself uphill till my feet were out, not just for a minute or two. But I would, I thought, given time.

The man came back, and brought a friend. Ungrateful of me to have misjudged him.

The companion peered through the rain and said, 'You are English? Did you say you are English?' His tone seemed to suggest that being English automatically explained such follies as swimming in October in shirt and underpants and lying about on slipways.

'Yes,' I said.

'You fell off a ship?'

'Sort of.'

I felt his hand slide under my armpit.

'Come. Out of the water.'

I scraped myself on to the slipway and with their help more or less crawled to the top. The quay was edged with railings and posts. I sat on the ground with my back against one of the posts and wished for enough strength to stand up.

They consulted in Norwegian. Then the English speaking one said, 'We will take you to my house, to dry and get warm.'

'Thank you,' I said, and by God I meant it.

One of them went away again and came back with a battered old van. They gave me the front passenger seat though I offered to drip in the back, and whisked me about a quarter of a mile to a small wooden house, standing near two or three others. There was no village, no shops, no telephone.

'This is an island,' my rescuer explained. 'One kilometre long, three hundred metres across.' He told me its name, which seemed to me like 'gorse'.

His living-room was small and bright, and warmed by the huge stove which took up at least a sixth of the floorspace. Seen clearly in the light he himself was a short friendly man of middle age with hands that were used for work. He shook his head over me and produced first a blanket and then, after some rummaging, a thick woollen shirt and a pair of trousers.

'You are not a sailor,' he said matter of factly, watching me fumble off my shirt and pants.

'No,' I agreed.

My wallet fell on the floor. I was surprised it was still there; had forgotten it. The Norwegian-only rescuer politely picked it up and handed it to me, smiling broadly. He looked very like his friend.

Between hopeless bouts of shivering I told them what had happened and asked them how I could get back to the city. They talked to each other about it while I dressed, first with a lot of shaking of heads but finally with a few nods.

'When you are warmer we will take you by boat,' said the English-speaker. He looked at the wallet which lay now on a polished pine table. 'We ask only that you will pay for the fuel. If you can.'

Together we took out my sodden money and spread it on the table. I asked them to take whatever they liked, and after debate they chose a fifty kroner note. I urged them to double it. It wouldn't cost so much, they protested, but in the end they put two notes aside and dried the rest for me quickly on the stove so that the edges curled. After more consultation they dug in a cupboard and brought out a bottle of pale gold liquid. One small glass followed, and a moderate tot was poured into it. They handed it to me.

'*Skol!*' they said.

'*Skol!*' I repeated.

They watched interestedly while I drank. Smooth fire down the throat, heat in the stomach, and soon a warm glow along all the frozen veins.

They smiled.

'Aquavit,' said my host, and stored the precious bottle away ready for the next needy stranger who swam to their doorstep.

They suggested I should sit for a while on the one comfortable-looking chair. Since various muscles were still trembling with weakness this seemed a good idea, so I rested while they busied themselves putting out businesslike sets of oilskins, and by the time they were kitted up my skin had returned from a nasty bluish purplish white to its more usual shade of sallow.

'D'you feel better?' my host observed, smiling.

'I do.'

They nodded, pleased, and held out a spare set of oilskins for me to put on. They took me in a big smelly fishing boat back up the twinkle-edged fjord to the city, and it rained all the way. I spent the journey calculating that I had been in the water for about two hours, which didn't prove anything in particular about the current in the fjord or the inefficiency of my swimming or the distance I had travelled, but did prove pretty conclusively that the temperature was more than one degree above freezing.

CHAPTER TWO

They waited while I changed at the Grand, so that they could take back the lent clothes. We parted with warm handshakes and great camaraderie, and it was only after they had gone that I realized that I didn't know their names.

I would have liked nothing better than to go to bed and sleep for half a century, but the thought of Arne's wife waiting for him to come home put a damper on that. So I spent the next couple of hours with various Norwegian authorities, reporting what had happened.

When the police finished taking notes and said they would send someone to tell Mrs Kristiansen, I suggested that I should go too. They agreed. We went in an official car and rang the bell of Flat C on the first floor of a large timber house in a prosperous road not far from the city centre.

The girl who opened the door looked inquiringly out at us from clear grey eyes in a firm, friendly, thirtyish face. Behind her the flat looked warm and colourful, and the air was thick with Beethoven.

19

'Is Mrs Kristiansen in?' I asked.

'Yes,' she said. 'I am Mrs Kristiansen.'

Not in the least what I would have expected. Oddballs like Arne shouldn't turn out to have slender young wives with thick pale blonde hair falling in loose curls on their shoulders. She looked away from my own less striking face to the policeman behind me, and the eyes widened.

'I'm David Cleveland,' I said. 'I was with Arne this afternoon . . .'

'Oh were you?' she exclaimed. 'Oh, do come in . . . I'm *so* glad . . .'

She held the door wider and turned to call over her shoulder.

'Arne,' she said. 'Arne, see who's here.'

He stepped into the hall. Very much alive.

We stared at each other in consternation. My own face must have mirrored the surprise and shock I saw on his, and then he was striding forward with his hand outheld and his face creasing into the most gigantic smile of all time.

'David! I don't believe it. I have reported you drowned.' He clasped both my hands in both of his and shook them warmly. 'Come in, come in, my dear fellow, and tell me how you were saved. I have been so grieved . . . I was telling Kari . . .'

His wife nodded, as delighted as he was.

The policeman behind me said, 'It would seem Mr Kristiansen wasn't drowned after all, then,' which seemed in our high state of relief to be extremely funny. We all laughed. Even the policeman smiled.

'I was picked up by some fisherman near Nesodden,' Arne told him. 'I reported the accident to the police there. They said they would send a boat to look for Mr Cleveland, but they weren't very hopeful of finding him. I'd better call them . . .'

'Thank you,' said the policeman. 'That would be helpful,' and he smiled once more at us all and went away.

Kari Kristiansen shut the front door and said 'Do come in, we must celebrate,' and led me through into the living-room. Beethoven was thundering away in there, and Kari switched him off. 'Arne always plays loud music when he's upset,' she said.

Out in the hall Arne busied himself with the telephone, and among his explanatory flow of Norwegian I caught my own name spoken with astonishment and relief.

'It is wonderful,' he said, coming into the room and rubbing his hands together. 'Wonderful.' He gestured to me to sit on a deep comfortable sofa near a cheerful wood-burning fire. 'The Nesodden police say they sent a boat out to search for you, but it was too dark and raining and they could see nothing.'

'I'm sorry they had the trouble,' I said.

'My dear fellow . . .' He spread his fingers. 'It was nothing. And now, a drink, eh? To celebrate.'

He filled glasses of red wine from a bottle standing already open on a side-table.

'Arne has been so depressed all evening,' Kari said. 'It is truly a miracle that you were both saved.'

We exchanged stories. Arne had torn off the red clothes and kicked his boots off instantly (I suppose I should have known that a man at home on the sea would wear *loose* gumboots), but although he had called my name and searched around for some minutes he had caught no sign of me.

'When I last saw you,' he said apologetically, 'you were still in the dinghy, and I thought the speedboat must have hit you directly, so when I could not see you I thought that you must be already dead.'

He had started swimming, he said; and knowing a lot more than I did about tides and winds, had taken almost the opposite direction. He had been picked up near the coast by a small home-going fishing boat which was too low on fuel to go out into the fjord to look for me. It had however landed him in the small town where he reported my loss, and from there he had returned by hired boat to the city.

My story was so much the same that it could be told in two sentences: I swam to an island. Two men brought me back in a boat.

Arne searched among an untidy pile of papers and triumphantly produced a map. Spreading it out, he pointed to the widest part of the fjord and showed both Kari and me where we had sunk.

'The worst possible place,' Kari exclaimed. 'Why did you go so far?'

'You know me,' said Arne, folding the map up again. 'I like to be moving.'

She looked at him indulgently. 'You don't like to be followed, you mean.'

Arne looked a little startled, but that complex of his stood out like Gulliver in Lilliput.

I said, 'The police asked me if I saw the name of that speedboat.'

'Did you?' asked Arne.

I shook my head. 'No. Did you?'

He blinked through one of those maddening pauses into which the simplest question seemed to throw him, but in the end all he said was 'No, I didn't.'

'I don't think there was any name to see,' I said.

They both turned their faces to me in surprise.

'There must have been,' Kari said.

'Well . . . I've no impression of one . . . no name, no registration number, no port of origin. Perhaps you don't have things like that in Norway.'

'Yes we do,' Kari said, puzzled. 'Of course we do.'

Arne considered lengthily, then said, 'It was going too fast . . . and straight towards us. It must have had a name. We simply didn't see it.' He spoke with finality, as if the subject could hold no more interest. I nodded briefly and let it go, but I was certain that on that thundering black hull there had been nothing to see but black paint. How were they off for smugglers, I wondered, in this neck of the North Sea?

'It's a pity,' I said. 'Because you might have got compensation for your dinghy.'

'It was insured,' he said. 'Do not worry.'

Kari said, 'It's disgraceful he did not stop. He must have felt the bump . . . even a big heavy speedboat, like Arne says it was, could not crush a dinghy without feeling it.'

Hit and run, I thought flippantly. Happens on the roads, why not on the water?

'Arne was afraid you could not swim.'

'Up and down a pool or two,' I said. 'Never tried such long-distance stuff before.'

'You were lucky,' she said seriously.

'Arne too.' I looked at him thoughtfully, for I was younger by a good ten years and I had been near to exhaustion.

'Oh no. Arne's a great swimmer. A great sportsman, all round. Very fit and tough.' She smiled ironically, but the wifely pride was there. 'He used to win across-country ski races.'

There had been several sets of skis stacked casually in an alcove in the hall, along with squash rackets, fishing rods, mountain walking boots and half a dozen anoraks like the lost red one. For a man who liked to keep moving, he had all the gear.

'Have you eaten?' Kari asked suddenly. 'Since your swim, I mean? Did you think of eating?'

24

I shook my head.

'I suppose I was worried about Arne.'

She stood up, smiling. 'Arne had no appetite for his supper.' She looked at the clock. Ten minutes before ten. 'I will bring something for you both,' she said.

Arne fondly watched her backview disappearing towards the kitchen.

'What do you think of her, eh? Isn't she beautiful?'

Normally I disliked men who invited admiration for their wives as if they were properties like cars, but I would have forgiven Arne a great deal that evening.

'Yes,' I said, more truthfully than on many similar occasions; and Arne positively smirked.

'More wine,' he said, getting up restlessly and filling both our glasses.

'Your house, too, is beautiful,' I said.

He looked over his shoulder in surprise. 'That is Kari as well. She ... it is her job. Making rooms for people. Offices, hotels. Things like that.'

Their own sitting-room was a place of natural wood and white paint, with big parchment-shaded table lamps shedding a golden glow on string-coloured upholstery and bright scattered cushions. A mixture of the careful and haphazard, overlaid with the comfortable debris of a full life. Ultra-tidy rooms always oppressed me: the Kristiansens' was just right.

Arne brought back my filled glass and settled himself opposite, near the fire. His hair, no longer hidden, was now more grey than blond; longer than before, and definitely more distinguished.

'Tomorrow,' I said, 'I'd like to see the racecourse Chairman, if I could.'

He looked startled, as if he had forgotten the real purpose of my visit.

'Yes.' He blinked a bit. 'It is Saturday tomorrow. It is the Grand National meeting on Sunday. He will be at the racecourse on Sunday.'

Don't let a thieving jockey spoil the man's day off, Arne was meaning, so I shrugged and said Sunday would do.

'I'll maybe call on Gunnar Holth tomorrow, then.'

For some reason that didn't fill Arne with joy either, but I discovered, after a long pause on his part, that this was because he, Arne, wished to go fishing all day and was afraid I would want him with me, instead.

'Does Gunnar Holth speak English?' I asked.

'Oh yes.'

'I'll go on my own, then.'

He gave me the big smile and jumped up to help Kari, who was returning with a laden tray. She had brought coffee and open sandwiches of prawns and cheese and pineapple which we ate to the last crumb.

'You must come another evening,' Kari said. 'I will make you a proper dinner.'

Arne agreed with her warmly and opened some more wine.

'A great little cook,' he said proprietorially.

The great little cook shook back her heavy blonde hair and stretched her elegant neck. She had a jaw-line in the same class and three small brown moles like dusty freckles high on one cheekbone.

'Come any time,' she said.

I got back to the Grand by taxi at one in the morning, slept badly, and woke at seven feeling like Henry Cooper's punchbag.

Consultation with the bathroom looking-glass revealed a plate-sized bruise of speckled crimson over my left shoulder-blade, souvenir of colliding boats. In addition every muscle I possessed was groaning with the morning-after misery of too much strain. David Cleveland, it seemed, was no Matthew Webb.

Bath, clothes and breakfast didn't materially improve things, nor on the whole did a telephone call to Gunnar Holth.

'Come if you like,' he said. 'But I can tell you nothing. You will waste your time.'

As all investigators waste a lot of time listening to people with nothing to tell, I naturally went. He had a stable yard adjoining the racecourse and a belligerent manner.

'Questions, questions,' he said. 'There is nothing to tell.'

I paid off my taxi driver.

'You shouldn't have sent him away,' Gunnar Holth said. 'You will be going soon.'

I smiled. 'I can go back on a tram.'

He gave me a grudging stare. 'You don't look like a Jockey Club official.'

'I would appreciate it very much,' I said, 'if you would show me your horses. Arne Kristiansen says you have a good lot . . . that they've been winning big prizes this year.'

He loosened, of course. He gestured towards a large barn on the other side of an expanse of mud. We made our way there, him in his boots showing me I shouldn't have come in polished shoes. He was short, wiry, middle-aged and a typical stableman, more at home with his horses, I guessed, than with their owners; and he spoke English with an Irish accent.

The barn contained two rows of boxes facing into a wide central passage. Horses' heads showed over most of the half doors and three or four lads were carrying buckets of water and haynets.

'They've just come in from exercise,' Holth said. 'We train on the sand track on the racecourse.' He turned left and opened the door of the first box. 'This fellow runs tomorrow in the Grand National. Would you look at his shoulders now, isn't that a grand sort of horse?'

'Bob Sherman won a race on him the day he disappeared,' I said.

He gave me a sharp wordless glance and went in to pat a strong-looking character with more bone than

28

breeding. He felt the legs, looked satisfied, and came back to join me.

'How do you know?' he said.

No harm in telling him. 'Arne Kristiansen gave me a list of Bob Sherman's last rides in Norway. He said that this horse of yours was likely to win the National, and if Sherman had had any sense he would have come back for that race and then stolen the National day takings, which would have been a better haul all round.'

Holth allowed himself a glint of amusement. 'That's true.'

We continued round the barn, admiring every inmate. There were about twenty altogether, three-quarters of them running on the flat, and although they seemed reasonable animals, none of them looked likely to take Epsom by storm. From their coats, though, and general air of well-being, Holth knew his trade.

One end of the barn was sectioned off to form living quarters for the lads, and Holth took me through to see them. Dormitory, washroom, and kitchen.

'Bob stayed here, most times,' he said.

I glanced slowly round the big main room with its half dozen two-tiered bunk beds, its bare board floor, its wooden table, wooden chairs. A big brown-tiled stove and double-glazed windows with curtains like blankets promised comfort against future snow, and a couple of mild girlie calendars brightened the walls, but it was a far cry from the Grand.

'Always?' I asked.

Holth shrugged. 'He said it was good enough here, and he saved the expense of a hotel. Nothing wrong there now, is there?'

'Nothing at all,' I agreed.

He paused. 'Sometimes he stayed with an owner.'

'Which owner?'

'Oh ... the man who owns Whitefire. Per Bjørn Sandvik.'

'How many times?'

Holth said with irritation, 'What does it matter? Twice, I suppose. Yes, twice. Not the last time. The two times before that.'

'How often did he come over altogether?'

'Six perhaps. Or seven ... or eight.'

'All this summer?'

'He didn't come last year, if that's what you mean.'

'But he liked it?'

'Of course he liked it. All British jockeys who are invited, they like it. Good pay, you see.'

'How good?'

'Well,' he said, 'They get their fare over here, and a bit towards expenses. And the fees for riding. And the appearance money.'

'The racecourse pays the appearance money?'

'Not exactly. Well ... the racecourse pays the money to the jockey but collects it from the owners who the jockey rode for.'

'So an owner, in the end, pays everything, the riding

fees, the winning percentage, a share of the fares, and a share of the appearance money?'

'That is right.'

'What happens if after all that the jockey rides a stinking race?'

Holth answered with deadly seriousness. 'The owner does not ask the jockey to come again.'

We stepped out of the barn back into the mud. It hadn't actually rained that day, but the threat still hung in the cold misty air.

'Come into my house,' suggested Holth. 'Have some coffee before you catch the tram.'

'Great,' I said.

His house was a small wooden bungalow with lace curtains and geraniums in pots on every window sill. The stove in the living-room was already lit, with an orange metal coffee pot heating on top. Gunnar dug into a cupboard for two earthenware mugs and some sugar in a packet.

'Would the owners have asked Bob Sherman to come again?' I said.

He poured the coffee, stirring with a white plastic spoon.

'Per Bjørn Sandvik would. And Sven Wangen; that's the owner of that dappled mare on the far side.' He pondered. 'Rolf Torp, now. Bob lost a race the day he went. Rolf Torp thought he should have walked it.'

'And should he?'

Holth shrugged. 'Horses aren't machines,' he said.

'Mind you, I don't train Rolf Torp's horses, so I don't really know, do I?'

'Who trains them?'

'Paul Sundby.'

'Will Rolf Torp be at the races tomorrow?'

'Naturally,' Holth said. 'He has the favourite in the National.'

'And you,' I said. 'Would you have asked him to ride for you again?'

'Certainly,' he said without hesitation. 'Bob is a good jockey. He listens to what you say about a horse. He rides with his head. He would not have been asked so many times if he had not been good.'

The door from the yard opened without warning and one of the lads poked his head in: he was about twenty-five, cheerful, and wore a woollen cap with a pompom.

'Gunny,' he said, 'will ye be takin' a look at that bleedin' mare now? She's a right cow, that one.'

The trainer said he would look in a minute, and the head withdrew.

'He's Irish,' I said surprised.

'Sure. I've three Irish lads and one from Yorkshire. And three from here. There's a lot of British lads in Norwegian racing.'

'Why is that?'

'They get a chance of riding in races here, see? More than they do at home.'

We drank the coffee which was well boiled and all the stronger for it.

I said, 'What did Bob do for transport? Did he ever hire a car?'

'No. I don't think so. When he stayed here he used to go with me over to the course.'

'Did he ever borrow your car? Or anyone's?'

'He didn't borrow mine. I don't think he ever drove, when he came.'

'Did you take him anywhere except to the races, the day he disappeared?'

'No.'

I knew from a file of statements which had been awaiting my arrival at the hotel that Bob Sherman had been expected to leave the racecourse by taxi to catch the late flight to Heathrow. He had not caught it. The taxi driver who had been engaged for the trip had simply shrugged when his passenger didn't show, and had taken some ordinary race-goers back to the city instead.

That left public transport, all the taxi drivers who didn't know Bob by sight, and other people's cars. Plus, I supposed, his own two feet. It would have been all too easy to leave the racecourse without being seen by anyone who knew him, particularly if, as the collected notes implied, the last race had been run after dark.

I put down my empty coffee mug and Gunnar Holth abruptly said, 'Could you be doing something about Bob's wife, now?'

'His wife? I might see her when I go back, if I find out anything useful.'

'No,' he shook his head. 'She is here.'

'Here?'

He nodded. 'In Oslo. And she won't go home.'

'Arne didn't mention it.'

Holth laughed. 'She follows him round like a dog. She asks questions, like you. Who saw Bob go, who did he go with, why does no one find him? She comes to every race meeting and asks and asks. Everyone is very tired of it.'

'Do you know where she's staying?'

He nodded vigorously and picked up a piece of paper lying near on a shelf.

'The Norsland Hotel. Second class, away from the centre. This is her telephone number. She gave it to me in case I could think of anything to help.' He shrugged. 'Everyone is sorry for her. But I wish she would go away.'

'Will you telephone her?' I said. 'Say I would like to ask her some questions about Bob. Suggest this afternoon.'

'I've forgotten your name,' he said without apology.

I smiled and gave him one of the firm's official cards. He looked at it and me in disbelief, but got the Norsland Hotel on the line. Mrs Emma Sherman was fetched.

Holth said into the receiver, 'A Mr David Cleveland ... come from England to try to find your husband.' He read from the card, 'Chief Investigator, Investigation Office, Jockey Club, Portman Square, London. He wants to see you this afternoon.'

He listened to the reaction, then looked at me and said 'Where?'

'At her hotel. Three o'clock.'

He relayed the news.

'She'll be waiting for you,' he said, putting the receiver down.

'Good.'

'Tell her to go home,' he said.

CHAPTER THREE

She was waiting in the small lobby of the Norsland, sitting on the edge of a chair and anxiously scanning the face of every passing male. I watched her for a while through the glass doors to the street, before going in. She looked small and pale and very very jumpy. Twice she half stood up, and twice, as the man she had focused on walked past without a sign, subsided more slowly back to her seat.

I pushed through the doors into air barely warmer than the street, which in a totally centrally heated city spoke poorly of the management. Emma Sherman looked at me briefly and switched her gaze back to the door. I was not what she expected: the next man through, sixtyish and military-looking, had her again halfway to her feet.

He passed her without a glance on his way to collect his room key at the desk. She sat slowly down, looking increasingly nervous.

I walked over to her.

'Mrs Sherman?'

'Oh.' She stood up slowly. 'Is there a message from Mr Cleveland?'

'I am,' I said, 'David Cleveland.'

'But,' she said, and stopped. The surprise lingered on her face among the strain and tiredness, but she seemed past feeling anything very clearly. At close quarters the nervousness resolved itself into a state not far from total breakdown.

Her skin looked almost transparent from fatigue, dark shadows round her eyes emphasizing the pebbly dullness of the eyes themselves. She was about twenty-two and should have been pretty: she had the bones and the hair for it, but they hadn't a chance. She was also, it seemed to me, pregnant.

'Where can we talk?' I asked.

She looked vaguely round the lobby which contained three chairs, no privacy, and a rubber plant.

'Your room?' I suggested.

'Oh no,' she said at once, and then more slowly, in explanation, 'It is small . . . not comfortable . . . nowhere to sit.'

'Come along, then,' I said. 'We'll find a coffee shop.'

She came with me out into the street and we walked in the general direction of the Grand.

'Will you find him?' she said. 'Please find him.'

'I'll do my best.'

'He never stole that money,' she said. 'He didn't.'

I glanced at her. She was trembling perceptibly and looking paler than ever. I stopped walking and put my hand under her elbow. She looked at me with glazing eyes, tried to say something else, and fell forward against me in a thorough-going swoon.

Even seven stone nothing of fainting girl is hard to support without letting her lie on a cold city pavement. Two passing strangers proved to have friendly faces but no English, and the third, who had the tongue, muttered something about the disgrace of being drunk at four in the afternoon and scurried away. I held her up against me with my arms under hers and asked the next woman along to call a taxi.

She too looked disapproving and backed away, but a boy of about sixteen gave her a withering glance and came to the rescue.

'Is she ill?' he asked. His English was punctilious stuff, learned in school.

'She is. Can you get a taxi?'

'*Ja.* I will return. You will . . .' he thought, then found the word . . . 'Wait?'

'I will wait,' I agreed.

He nodded seriously and darted away round the nearest corner, a slim figure in the ubiquitous uniform of the young, blue jeans and a padded jacket. He came back, as good as his word, with a taxi, and helped me get the girl into it.

'Thank you very much,' I said.

He beamed. 'I learn English,' he said.

'You speak it very well.'

He waved as the taxi drew away: a highly satisfactory encounter to both parties.

She began to wake up during the short journey, which seemed to reassure the taxi driver. He spoke no English except one word which he repeated at least ten times with emphasis, and which was 'doctor'.

'*Ja*,' I agreed. '*Ja*. At the Grand Hotel.'

He shrugged, but drove us there. He also helped me support her through the front doors and accepted his fare after she was safely sitting down.

'Doctor,' he said as he left, and I said, '*Ja*.'

'No,' said Bob Sherman's wife, in little more than a whisper. 'What . . . happened?'

'You fainted,' I said briefly. 'And doctor or no doctor, you need to lie down. So up you come . . .' I more or less lifted her to her feet, walked her to the lift, and took her up the one floor to my room. She flopped full length on the bed without question and lay there with her eyes closed.

'Do you mind if I feel your pulse?' I asked.

She gave no answer either way, so I put my fingers on her wrist and found the slow heartbeat. Her arm was slippery with sweat though noticeably cold, and all in all she looked disturbingly frail.

'Are you hungry?' I said.

She rolled her head on the pillow in a slow negative, but I guessed that what was really wrong with her, besides strain, was simple starvation. She had been too

39

worried to take care of herself, and besides, eating came expensive in Norway.

A consultation on the telephone with the hotel restaurant produced a promise of hot meat soup and some bread and cheese.

'And brandy,' I said.

'No brandy, sir, on Saturday. Or on Sunday. It is the rule.'

I had been warned, but had forgotten. Extraordinary to find a country with madder licensing laws than Britain's. There was a small refrigerator in my room, however, which stocked, among the orangeade and mineral waters, a quarter bottle of champagne. It had always seemed to me that bottling in quarters simply spoiled good fizz, but there's an occasion for everything. Emma said she couldn't, she shouldn't; but she did, and within five minutes was looking like a long-picked flower caught just in time.

'I'm sorry,' she said, leaning on one elbow on my bed and sipping the golden bubbles from my tooth mug.

'You're welcome.'

'You must think me a fool.'

'No.'

'It's just . . . No one seems to care any more. Where he's gone. They just say they can't find him. They aren't even looking.'

'They've looked,' I began, but she wasn't ready to listen.

'Then Gunnar Holth said . . . the Jockey Club had sent their chief investigator . . . so I've been hoping so hard all day that at last someone would find him, and then . . . and then . . . you . . .'

'I'm not the father-figure you were hoping for,' I said.

She shook her head. 'I didn't think you'd be so young.'

'Which do you want most,' I asked. 'A father-figure, or someone to find Bob?' But it was too soon to expect her to see that the two things didn't necessarily go together. She needed the comfort as much as the search.

'He didn't steal that money,' she said.

'How do you know?'

'He just wouldn't.' She spoke with conviction, but I wondered if the person she most wanted to convince was herself.

A waiter knocked on the door, bringing a tray, and Emma felt well enough to sit at the table and eat. She started slowly, still in a weak state, but by the end it was clear she was fiercely hungry.

As she finished the last of the bread I said, 'In about three hours we'll have dinner.'

'Oh no.'

'Oh yes. Why not? Then you'll have plenty of time to tell me about Bob. Hours and hours. No need to hurry.'

She looked at me with the first signs of connected

41

thought and almost immediately glanced round the room. The awareness that she was in my bedroom flashed out like neon in the North Pole. I smiled. 'Would you prefer the local nick? One each side of a table in an interview room?'

'Oh! I . . . suppose not.' She shuddered slightly. 'I've had quite a lot of that, you see. In a way. Everyone's been quite kind, really, but they think Bob stole that money and they treat me as if my husband was a crook. It's . . . it's pretty dreadful.'

'I understand that,' I said.

'Do you?'

The meal had done nothing for her pallor. The eyes still looked as hollowed and black-smudged, and the strain still vibrated in her manner. It was going to take more than champagne and soup to undo the knots.

'Why don't you sleep for a while?' I suggested. 'You look very tired. You'll be quite all right here, and I've some reports which I ought to write. I'd be glad to get them out of the way.'

'I can't sleep,' she said automatically, but when I determinedly took papers out of my briefcase, spread them on the table and switched on a bright lamp to see them by, she stood up and hovered a bit and finally lay down again on the bed. After five minutes I walked over to look and she was soundly asleep with sunken cheeks and pale blue veins in her eyelids.

She wore a camel coloured coat, which she had relaxed as far as unbuttoning, and a brown and white checked dress underneath. With the coat falling open, the bulge in her stomach showed unmistakably. Five months, I thought, give or take a week or two.

I pushed the papers together again and returned them to the briefcase. They were the various statements and accounts relating to her husband's disappearance, and I had no report to write on them. I sat instead in one of the Grand's comfortable armchairs and thought about why men vanished.

In the main they either ran *to* something or *from* something: occasionally a combination of both. To a woman; from a woman. To the sunshine; from the police. To political preference; from political oppression. To anonymity; from blackmail.

Sometimes they took someone else's money with them to finance the future. Bob Sherman's sixteen thousand kroner didn't seem, at first sight, to be worth what he'd exchanged for it. He earned five times as much every year.

So what had he gone *to*?

Or what had he gone *from*?

And how was I to find him by Monday afternoon?

She slept soundly for more than two hours with periods of peaceful dreaming, but after that went into a session which was distressing her. She moved restlessly and sweat appeared on her forehead, so I touched her hand and called her out of it.

'Emma. Wake up. Wake up, now, Emma.'

She opened her eyes fast and wide with the night-mare pictures still in them. Her body began to tremble.

'Oh,' she said. 'Oh God . . .'

'It's all right. You were dreaming. It was only a dream.'

Her mind finished the transition to consciousness, but she was neither reassured nor comforted.

'I dreamed he was in jail . . . there were bars . . . and he was trying to get out . . . frantically . . . and I asked him why he wanted to get out, and he said they were going to execute him in the morning . . . and then I was talking to someone in charge and I said what had he done, why were they going to execute him, and this man said . . . he'd stolen the racecourse . . . and the law said that if people stole racecourses they had to be executed . . .'

She rubbed a hand over her face.

'It's so silly,' she said. 'But it seemed so real.'

'Horrid,' I said.

She said with desolation, 'But where is he? Why doesn't he write to me? How can he be so cruel?'

'Perhaps there's a letter waiting at home.'

'No. I telephone . . . every day.'

I said, 'Are you . . . well . . . are you happy together?'

'Yes,' she said firmly, but after five silent seconds the truer version came limping out. 'Sometimes we have rows. We had one the day he came here. All morning. And it was over such a little thing . . . just that he'd spent a night away when he didn't have to ... I'd not been feeling well and I told him he was selfish and thoughtless ... and he lost his temper and said I was too damn demanding ... and I said I wouldn't go with him to Kempton then, and he went silent and sulky because he was going to ride the favourite in the big race and he always likes to have me there after something like that, it helps him unwind.' She stared into a past moment she would have given the world to change. 'So he went on his own. And from there to Heathrow for the six-thirty to Oslo, same as usual. Only usually I went with him, to see him off and take the car home.'

'And meet him again Sunday night?'

'Yes. On Sunday night when he didn't come back at the right time I was worried sick that he'd had a fall in Norway and hurt himself and I telephoned to Gunnar Holth ... but he said Bob hadn't fallen, he'd ridden a winner and got round in the other two races, and as far as he knew he'd caught the plane as planned. So I rang the airport again ... I'd rung them before, and they said the plane had landed on time ... and I begged them to check and they said there was no Sherman on the passenger list ...' She stopped and I waited, and she went on in a fresh onslaught of misery. 'Surely he knew I didn't really mean it? I love him ... Surely he wouldn't just leave me, without saying a word?'

It appeared, however, that he had.

'How long have you been married?'

'Nearly two years.'

'Children?'

She glanced down at the brown and white checked mound and gestured towards it with a flutter of slender fingers. 'This is our first.'

'Finances?'

'Oh . . . all right, really.'

'How really?'

'He had a good season last year. We saved a bit then. Of course he does like good suits and a nice car . . . All jockeys do, don't they?'

I nodded. I knew also more about her husband's earnings than she seemed to, as I had access to the office which collected and distributed jockeys' fees; but it wasn't so much the reasonable income that was significant as the extent to which they lived within it.

'He does get keen on schemes for making money quickly, but we've never lost much. I usually talk him out of it. I'm not a gambler at all, you see.'

I let a pause go by. Then, 'Politics?'

'How do you mean?'

'Is he interested in communism?'

She stared. 'Good heavens, no.'

'Militant in any way?'

She almost laughed. 'Bob doesn't give a damn for politics or politicians. He says they're all the same, hot air and hypocrisy. Why do you ask such an extraordinary question?'

I shrugged. 'Norway has a common frontier with Russia.'

Her surprise was genuine on two counts: she didn't know her geography and she did know her husband. He was not the type to exchange good suits and a nice car and an exciting job for a dim existence in a totalitarian state.

'Did he mention any friends he had made here?'

'I've seen nearly everyone I can remember him talking about. I've asked them over and over ... Gunnar Holth, and his lads, and Mr Kristiansen, and the owners. The only one I haven't met is one of the owner's sons, a boy called Mikkel. Bob mentioned him once or twice ... he's away at school now, or something.'

'Was Bob in any trouble before this?'

She looked bewildered. 'What sort?'

'Bookmakers?'

She turned her head away and I gave her time to decide on her answer. Jockeys were not allowed to bet, and I worked for the Jockey Club.

'No,' she said indistinctly.

'You might as well tell me,' I said. 'I can find out. But you would be quicker.'

She looked back at me, perturbed. 'He only bets on himself, usually,' she said defensively. 'It's legal in a lot of countries.'

'I'm only interested in his betting if it's got anything to do with his disappearance. Was anyone threatening him for payment?'

'Oh.' She sounded forlorn, as if the one thing she

did not want to be given was a good reason for Bob to steal a comparatively small sum and ruin his life for it.

'He never said . . . I'm sure he would have told . . .' She gulped. 'The police asked me if he was being blackmailed. I said no, of course not . . . but if it was to keep me from knowing something . . . how can I be sure? Oh, I do wish, I do wish he'd write to me . . .'

Tears came in a rush and spilled over. She didn't apologize, didn't brush them away, and in a few seconds they had stopped. She had wept a good deal, I guessed, during the past three weeks.

'You've done all you can here,' I said. 'Better come back with me on Monday afternoon.'

She was surprised and disappointed. 'You're going back so soon? But you won't have found him.'

'Probably not. But I've a meeting in London on Tuesday that I can't miss. If it looks like being useful I'll come back here afterwards, but for you, it's time now to go home.'

She didn't answer at once, but finally, in a tired, quiet, defeated voice, said 'All right.'

CHAPTER FOUR

Arne was having difficulty with his complex, constantly looking over his shoulder to the extent of making forward locomotion hazardous. Why he should find any threat in the cheerful frost-bitten looking crowd which had turned up at Øvrevoll for the Norsk Grand National was something between him and his psychiatrist, but as usual his friends were suffering from his affliction.

He had refused, for instance, to drink a glass of wine in a comfortable available room with a king-sized log fire. Instead we were marching back and forth outside, him, me, and Per Bjørn Sandvik, wearing out shoe leather and turning blue at the ears, for fear of bugging machines. I couldn't see how overhearing our present conversation could possibly benefit anyone, but then I wasn't Arne. And at least this time, I thought philosophically, we would not be mown down by a speedboat.

As before, he was ready for the outdoor life: a blue padded hood joined all in one to his anorak. Per Bjørn

49

Sandvik had a trilby. I had my head. Maybe one day I would learn.

Sandvik, one of the Stewards, was telling me again at first hand what I'd already read in the statements: how Bob Sherman had had access to the money.

'It's collected into the officials' room, you see, where it is checked and recorded. And the officials' room is in the same building as the jockeys' changing-room. Right? And that Sunday, Bob Sherman went to the officials' room to ask some question or other, and the money was stacked there, just inside the door. Arne saw him there himself. He must have planned at once to take it.'

'What was the money contained in?' I asked.

'Canvas bags. Heavy double canvas.'

'What colour?'

He raised his eyebrows. 'Brown.'

'Just dumped on the floor?'

He grinned. 'There is less crime in Norway.'

'So I've heard,' I said. 'How many bags?'

'Five.'

'Heavy?'

He shrugged. 'Like money.'

'How were they fastened?'

'With leather straps and padlocks.'

Arne cannoned into a blonde who definitely had the right of way. She said something which I judged from his expression to be unladylike, but it still didn't persuade him to look where he was going. Some enemy lay behind, listening: he was sure of it.

Sandvik gave him an indulgent smile. He was a tall pleasant unhurried man of about fifty, upon whom authority sat as lightly as fluff. Arne had told me he was 'someone at the top in oil', but he had none of the usual aura of big business: almost the reverse, as if he derived pleasure from leaving an impression of no power, no aggression. If so, he would be a board-room opponent as wicked as a mantrap among the daisies. I looked at him speculatively. He met my eyes. Nothing in his that shouldn't be.

'What was it intended to do with the bags, if Sherman hadn't nicked them?' I asked.

'Lock them in the safe in the officials' room until Monday morning, when they would go to the bank.'

'Guarded,' Arne said, eyes front for once, 'By a night watchman.'

But by the time the night watchman had clocked in, the booty had vanished.

'How did the officials all happen to desert the room at once, leaving the money so handy?' I asked.

Sandvik spread his thickly gloved hands. 'We have discussed this endlessly. It was accidental. The room can only have been empty for five minutes or less. There was no special reason for them all being out at one time. It just happened.'

He had a high-register voice with beautifully distinct enunciation, but his almost-perfect English sounded quite different from the home-grown variety. I worked it out after a while: it was his 'l's. The British pronounced 'l' with their tongue lolling back in the throat, the Norwegians said theirs with the tongue tight up behind the teeth. Retaining the Norwegian 'l' gave Sandvik's accent a light, dry, clear-vowelled quality which made everything he said sound logical and lucid.

'No one realized, that evening, that the money had been stolen. Each of the officials took it for granted that another had put the bags in the safe as they were no longer to be seen. It was the next day, when the safe was opened for the money to be banked, that it was found to be missing. And then, of course, we heard from Gunnar Holth that Sherman had disappeared as well.'

I thought. 'Didn't Gunnar Holth tell me that Bob Sherman stayed with you once or twice?'

'Yes, that's right.' Sandvik briefly pursed his well-shaped mouth. 'Twice. But not the time he stole the money, I'm glad to say.'

'You liked him, though?'

'Oh yes, well enough, I suppose. I asked him out of politeness. He had ridden several winners for me, and I know what Gunnar's bunk room is like . . .' He grinned slightly. 'Anyway, he came. But we had little of common interest except horses, and I think he really preferred Gunnar's after all.'

'Would you have expected him to steal?'

'It never crossed my mind. I mean, it doesn't does it? But I didn't know him well.'

Arne could not bear the close quarters of the crowd on the stands, so we watched the first race, a hurdle, from rising ground just past the winning post. The race-course, forming the floor of a small valley, was overlooked on all sides by hillsides of spruce and birch, young trees growing skywards like the Perpendicular period come to life. The slim, dark evergreens stood in endless broken vertical stripes with the yellow-drying leaves and silver trunks of the birch, and the whole backdrop, that afternoon, was hung along the skyline with fuzzy drifts of misty low cloud.

The light was cold grey, the air cold damp. The spirits of the crowd, sunny Mediterranean. An English jockey won the race on the favourite and the crowd shouted approval.

It was time, Sandvik said, to go and see the Chairman, who had not been able to manage us sooner on account of lunching a visiting ambassador. We went into the Secretariat building adjoining the grandstand, up some sporting print-lined stairs, and into a large room containing not only the Chairman but five or six supporting Stewards. Per Bjørn Sandvik walked in first, then me, then Arne pushing his hood back, and the Chairman went on looking inquiringly at the door, still waiting for me, so to speak, to appear. I sometimes wondered if it would help if I were fat, bald and bespec-tacled: if premature ageing might produce more confidence and belief than the thin-six-feet-with-brown-hair job did. I'd done a fair amount of living, one way or another, but it perversely refused to show.

'This is David Cleveland,' Sandvik said, and several pairs of eyes mirrored the same disappointment.

'How do you do,' I murmured gently to the Chairman, and held out my hand.

'Er . . .' He cleared his throat and recovered manfully. 'So glad you have come.'

I made a few encouraging remarks about how pleasant I found it in Norway and wondered if any of them knew that Napoleon was promoted General at twenty-four.

The Chairman, Lars Baltzersen, was much like his letters to my office, brief, polite and effective. It took him approximately ten seconds to decide I wouldn't have been given my job if I couldn't do it, and I saw no need to tell him that my boss had died suddenly, eighteen months earlier, and left the manager-elect in charge a lot sooner than anyone intended.

'You sound older on the telephone,' he said simply, and I said I'd been told so before, and that was that.

'Go anywhere you like on the racecourse,' he said. 'Ask anything . . . Arne can interpret for those who do not speak English.'

'Thank you.'

'Do you need anything else?'

Second sight, I thought; but I said, 'Perhaps, if possible, to see you again before I go at the end of the afternoon.'

'Of course. Of course. We all want to hear of your progress. We'll all gather here after the last race.'

Heads nodded dubiously, and I fully expected to justify their lowly expectations. Either briefed or bored or merely busy, they drifted away through the door, leaving only Arne and the Chairman behind.

'Some beer?' suggested Baltzersen.

Arne said yes and I said no. Despite the glow from a huge stove it was a cold day for hops.

'How far is it to the Swedish border?' I asked.

'By road, about eighty kilometres,' Baltzersen said.

'Any formalities there?'

He shook his head. 'Not for Scandinavians in their own cars. There are few inspections or customs. But none of the frontier posts remember an Englishman crossing on that evening.'

'I know. Not even as a passenger in a Norwegian car. Would he have been spotted if he'd gone across crouching under a rug on the floor behind the driver's seat?'

They pondered. 'Very probably not,' Baltzersen said, and Arne agreed.

'Can you think of anyone who might have taken him? Anyone he was close to here, either in business or friendship?'

'I do not know him well enough,' the Chairman said

regretfully, and Arne blinked a little and said Gunnar Holth, or maybe some of the lads who worked for him.

'Holth says he drove him only round to the races,' I said: but he would have had plenty of time to drive into Sweden and back before Emma Sherman had rung him up.

'Gunnar tells lies whenever it suits him,' Arne said.

Lars Baltzersen sighed. 'I'm afraid that is true.'

He had grey hair, neatly brushed, with a tidy face and unimaginative clothes. I was beginning to get the feel of Norwegian behaviour patterns, and he came into the very large category of sober, slightly serious people who were kind, efficient, and under little stress. Get-up-and-go was conspicuously absent, yet the job would clearly be done. The rat race taken at a walk. Very civilized.

There were other types, of course.

'The people I hate here,' Emma Sherman had said, 'are the drunks.'

I'd taken her to dinner in the hotel the evening before, and had listened for several hours, in the end, to details of her life with Bob, her anxieties, and her experiences in Norway.

'When I first came,' she said, 'I used to have dinner in the dining-room, and all these men used to come and ask if they could share my table. They were quite polite, but very very persistent. They wouldn't go away. The head waiter used to get rid of them for me. He told me they were drunk. They didn't really look it. They weren't rolling or anything.'

I laughed. 'Considering the price of alcohol here, you wouldn't think they could.'

'No,' she said. 'Anyway I stopped having dinner. I needed to make my money go as far as possible and I hated eating on my own.'

Arne said, 'Where do you want to go first?'

Arne came into a third group: the kinks. You find them everywhere.

'Weighing room, I should think.'

They both nodded in agreement. Arne pulled his hood back over his head and we went down into the raw outdoors. The crowd had swelled to what Arne described as 'very big', but there was still plenty of room. One of the greatest advantages of life in Norway, I guessed, was the small population. I had not so far in its leisurely capital seen a queue or a crush or anyone fighting to get anywhere first. As there always seemed to be room for all, why bother?

The officials checking tickets at the gates between different enclosures were all keen young men of about twenty, most of them blond also, all with blue armbands on their anoraks. They knew Arne, of course, but they checked my pass even though I was with him, the serious faces hardly lightening as they nodded me through. Lars Baltzersen had given me a five-by-three-inch card stamped all over with *adgang paddock, adgang stallomradet, adgang indre bane* and one or two other *adgangs*, and it looked as if I wouldn't get far if I lost it.

The weighing room, black wood walls, white paint, red tiled roof, lay on the far side of the parade ring, where the jockeys were already out for the second race. Everything looked neat, organized and pleasing, and despite an eye trained to spot trouble at five hundred paces in a thick fog, I couldn't see any. Even in racing, good nature prevailed. Several of the lads leading the horses round wore sweaters in the owner's colours, matching the jockey's; a good and useful bit of display I'd seen nowhere else. I commented on it to Arne.

'*Ja*,' he said. 'Many of the private stables do that now. It helps the crowd to know their colours.'

Between the paddock and the U-shaped weighing room buildings, and up into the U itself, there was a grassy area planted thickly with ornamental bushes. Everyone walking between weighing room and paddock had to detour either to one side or the other, along comparatively narrow paths: it made a change from the rolling acres of concrete at home but took up a lot of apology time.

Once inside the weighing room Arne forgot about bugging machines and introduced me rapidly to a stream of people, like the secretary, clerk of the course, clerk of the scales, without once looking over his shoulder. I shook hands and chatted a bit, but although they all knew I was looking for Bob Sherman, I couldn't see anyone feeling twitchy about my presence.

'Come this way, David,' Arne said, and took me down a side passage with an open door at the end leading out to the racecourse. A step or two before this door, Arne turned smartly right, and we found ourselves in the officials' room from which the money had been stolen. It was just an ordinary businesslike room, wooden walls, wooden floor, wooden tables acting as desks, wooden chairs. (With all those forests, what else?) There were pleasant, red checked curtains, first-class central heating, and in one corner, a no-nonsense safe.

Apart from us, there was no one there.

'That's all there is,' Arne said. 'The money bags were left on the floor . . .' he pointed, 'and the lists of totals from each collecting point were put on that desk, same as usual. We still have the lists.'

It had struck me several times that Arne felt no responsibility for the loss of the money, nor did anyone seem in the remotest way to blame him, but by even the most elementary requirements of a security officer, he'd earned rock bottom marks.

'Do you still have the same system,' I asked, 'with the bags?'

Arne gave me a look somewhere between amusement and hurt.

'No. Since that day, the bags are put immediately into the safe.'

'Who has the keys?'

'I have some, and the secretary, and the clerk of the course.'

'And each of you three thought one of the other two had stowed the money away safely?'

'That is right.'

We left the room and stepped out into the open air. Several jockeys, changed into colours for later races but with warm coats on at the moment, came along the passage and out through the same door, and they, Arne, and I climbed an outside staircase on to a small open stand attached to the side of the weighing room buildings. From there, a furlong or more from the winning post, we watched the second race.

Arne had begun looking apprehensively around again, though there were barely twenty on the stand. I found I had begun doing it myself: it was catching. It netted, however, the sight of an English jockey who knew me, and as everyone after the finish poured towards the stairs I arranged to fetch up beside him. Arne went on down the steps, but the jockey stopped when I touched his arm, and was easy to keep back.

'Hallo,' he said in surprise. 'Fancy seeing you here.'

'Came about Bob Sherman,' I explained.

I'd found that if I said straight out what I wanted to know, I got better results. No one wasted time wondering what I suspected them of, and if they weren't feeling on the defensive they talked more.

'Oh. I see. Found the poor bugger, then?'

'Not yet,' I said.

'Let him go, why don't you?'

Rinty Ranger knew Bob Sherman as well as anyone who'd been thrown together in the same small professional group for five years, but they were not especially close friends. I took this remark to be a general statement of sympathy for the fox and asked if he didn't think stealing the money had been a bloody silly thing to do.

'Too right,' he said. 'I'll bet he wished he hadn't done it, five minutes after. But that's Bob all over, smack into things without thinking.'

'Makes him a good jockey,' I said, remembering how he flung his heart over fences regardless.

Rinty grinned, his thin, sharp face looking cold above his sheepskin coat. 'Yeah. Done him no good this time, though.'

'What else has he done that was impulsive?'

'I don't know... Always full of get-rich-quick schemes like buying land in the Bahamas or backing crazy inventors, and I even heard him on about pyramid selling once, only we told him not to be such a bloody fool. I mean, it's hard enough to earn the stuff, you don't actually want to throw it down the drain.'

'Were you surprised when he stole the money?' I asked.

'Well of course I was, for Chrissakes. And even more by him doing a bunk. I mean, why didn't he just stash away the loot and carry on with business as usual?'

'Takes nerve,' I said, but of course that was just

what Bob Sherman had. 'Also the money was in heavy canvas bags which would take a lot of getting into. He wouldn't have had time to do that and catch his flight home.'

Rinty thought a bit but came up with nothing useful.

'Stupid bugger,' he said. 'Nice wife, kid coming, good job. You'd think he'd have more sense.' And I'd got as far as that myself.

'Anyway, he's done me a favour,' Rinty said. 'I've got his ride in this here Grand National.' He opened his sheepskin a fraction to show me the colours underneath. 'The owner, fellow called Torp, isn't best pleased with Bob on any account. Says he should've won at a canter that last day he was here. Says he threw it away, left it too late, came through too soon, should've taken the outside, didn't put him right at the water, you name it, Bob did it wrong.'

'He got another English jockey, though.'

'Oh sure. D'you know how many home-bred jump jocks there are here? About fifteen, that's all, and some of those are English or Irish. Lads they are mostly. You don't get many self-employed chaps, like us. There isn't enough racing here for that. You get them going to Sweden on Saturdays, they race there on Saturdays. Here Thursdays and Sundays. That's the lot. Mind you, they don't keep the jumpers to look at. They all run once a week at least, and as there are only four or five jump races a week – all the rest are flat – it makes life interesting.'

'Were you and Bob often over here together?'

'This year, three or four trips, I suppose. But I came last year too, which he didn't.'

'How long is a trip?'

He looked surprised. 'Only a day usually. We race in England Saturday afternoon, catch the six-thirty, race here Sunday, catch the late plane back if we can, otherwise the eight-fifteen Monday morning. Sometimes we fly here Sunday morning, but it's cutting it a bit fine. No margin for hold-ups.'

'Do you get to know people here well, in that time?'

'I suppose it sort of accumulates. Why?'

'Has Bob Sherman made any friendships here, would you say?'

'Good God. Well, no, not that I know of, but then likely as not I wouldn't know if he did. He knows a lot of trainers and owners, of course. Do you mean girls?'

'Not particularly. Were there any?'

'Shouldn't think so. He likes his missus.'

'Do you mind thinking fairly hard about it?'

He looked surprised. 'If you like.'

I nodded. He lengthened the focus of his gaze in a most satisfactory manner and really concentrated. I waited without pressure, watching the crowd. Young, it was, by British standards: at least half under thirty, half blond, all the youth dressed in anoraks of blue, red, orange and yellow in the sort of colourful haphazard uniformity that stage designers plan for the chorus.

Rinty Ranger stirred and brought his vision back to the present.

'I don't know . . . He stayed with Mr Sandvik a couple of times, and said he got on better with his son than the old man . . . I met him once, the son, that is, with Bob when they were chatting at the races . . . but I wouldn't say they were great friends or anything . . .'

'How old is he, roughly?'

'The son? Sixteen, seventeen. Eighteen maybe.'

'Anyone else?'

'Well . . . One of the lads at Gunnar Holth's. An Irish lad, Paddy O'Flaherty. Bob knows him well, because Paddy used to work for old Tasker Mason, where Bob was apprenticed. They were lads together, one time, you might say. Bob likes staying at Gunnar Holth's on account of Paddy, I think.'

'Do you know if Paddy has a car?'

'Haven't a clue. Why don't you ask him? He's bound to be here.'

'Were you here,' I asked, 'the day Bob disappeared?'

''Fraid not.'

'Well . . . Mm . . . anything you can think of which is not what you'd've expected?'

'What bloody questions! Let's see . . . can't think of anything . . . except that he left his saddle here.'

'Bob?'

'Yes. It's in the changing-room. And his helmet. He must have known, the silly sod, that he'd never be able to race anywhere in the world again, otherwise he'd never have left them.'

I moved towards the stairs. Rinty hadn't told me a great deal, but if there had been much to tell the police of one country or the other would have found Bob long ago. He followed me down, and I wished him good luck in the National.

'Thanks,' he said. 'Can't say I wish you the same, though. Let the poor bastard alone.'

At the bottom of the steps, Arne was talking to Per Bjørn Sandvik. They turned to include me with smiles, and I asked the offensive question with as much tact as possible.

'Your son Mikkel, Mr Sandvik. Do you think he could've driven Bob Sherman away from the races? Without knowing, of course, that he had the money with him?'

Per Bjørn reacted less violently than many a father would to the implication that his son, having entertained a thief even if unawares, had nonetheless kept quiet about it. Scarcely a ripple went through him.

He said smoothly, 'Mikkel cannot drive yet. He is still at school . . . his seventeenth birthday was six weeks ago.'

'That's good,' I said in apology; and I thought, that's that.

Per Bjørn said 'Excuse me,' without noticeable resentment and walked away. Arne, blinking furiously, asked where I wanted to go next. To see Paddy

O'Flaherty, I said, so we went in search and found him in the stables getting Gunnar Holth's runner ready for the Grand National. He turned out to be the lad in the woolly cap with uncomplimentary opinions of a mare, and described himself as Gunny's head lad, so I am.

'What did I do after the races?' he repeated. 'Same as I always do. Took the runners home, squared 'em up and saw to their scoff.'

'And after that?'

'After that, same as always, down to the local hop. There's a good little bird there, d'you see?'

'Do you have a car?' I asked.

'Well, sure I have now, but the tyres are as thin as a stockpot on Thursday and I wouldn't be after driving on them any more at all. And there's the winter coming on, so there's my car up on bricks, d'you see?'

'When did you put it on bricks?'

'The police stopped me about those tyres, now . . . well, there's the canvas peeping through one or two, if you look close. Sure it's all of six weeks ago now.'

After that we drifted around while I took in a general view of what went on, and then walked across the track to watch a race from the tower. This looked slightly like a small airfield control tower, two storeys high with a glass-walled room at the top. In this eyrie during races sat two keen-eyed men with fierce race-glasses clamped to their eyes: they were non-automatic patrol cameras, and never missed a trick.

Arne introduced me. Feel free, they said, smiling, to

come up into the tower at any time. I thanked them and stayed to watch the next race from there, looking straight down the narrow elongated oval of the track. Sixteen hundred metres for staying two-year-olds: they started almost level with the tower, scurried a long way away, rounded the fairly sharp bottom bend, and streamed up the long straight to finish at the winning post just below where we stood. There was a photo-finish. The all-seeing eyes unstuck themselves from their raceglasses, nodded happily, and said they would be back for the next race.

Before following them down the stairs I asked Arne which way the Grand National went, as there seemed to be fences pointing in every direction.

'Round in a figure of eight,' he said, sweeping a vague arm. 'Three times round. You will see when they go.' He seemed to want to be elsewhere fairly promptly, but when we had hurried back over to the paddock it appeared merely that he was hungry and had calculated enough eating time before the Norsk St Leger. He magicked some huge open sandwiches on about a foot of french loaf, starting at one end with prawns and proceeding through herring, cheese, pâté and egg to beef at the far end, adorned throughout by pickled cucumber, mayonnaise and scattered unidentified crispy bits. Arne stayed the course, but I blew up in the straight.

We drank wine: a bottle. We would come back later, Arne said, and finish it. We were in the big warm room he had shunned earlier, but the listeners weren't troubling him at that moment.

'If you're going home tomorrow, David,' he said, 'come to supper with us tonight.'

I hesitated. 'There's Emma Sherman,' I said.

'That girl,' he exclaimed. He peered around, though there were barely six others in the room. 'Where is she? She's usually on my heels.'

'I talked to her yesterday. Persuaded her not to come today and to go back to England tomorrow.'

'Great. Great, my friend.' He rubbed his hands together. 'She'll be all right, then. You come to supper with us. I will telephone to Kari.'

I thought of Kari's hair and Kari's shape. Everything stacked as I liked it best. I imagined her in bed. Very likely I should have allowed no such thoughts but you might as well forbid fish to swim. A pity she was Arne's, I thought. To stay away would make it easier on oneself.

'Come,' Arne said.

Weak, that's what I am. I said, 'I'd love to.'

He bustled off instantly to do the telephoning and soon returned beaming.

'She is very pleased. She says we will give you cloud-berries, she bought some yesterday.'

We went out to the raw afternoon and watched the big flat race together, but then Arne was whisked off on official business and for a while I wandered around alone. Though its organization and upkeep were clearly first class, it was not on British terms a big racecourse.

Plenty of room, but few buildings. Everyone could see: no one was pushed, rushed or crushed. Space was the ultimate luxury, I thought, as I strolled past a small oblong ornamental pond with a uniformed military band playing full blast beside it. Several children sat in bright little heaps around the players' feet and one or two were peering interestedly into the quivering business ends of trombones.

Øvrevoll, someone had told me, was a fairly new racecourse, the only one in Norway to hold ordinary flat and jump races. Most racing, as in Germany, was trotting, with sulkies.

For the Grand National itself I went back up the tower, which I found stood in the smaller top part of the figure of eight, with the larger part lying in the main part of the course, inside the flat track. Twenty runners set off at a spanking pace to go three and a half times round, which set the binocular men in the tower rotating like gyros. Soon after the start the horses circled the tower, cut closer across beside it and sped towards the water jump and the farther part of the course, took the bottom bend, and returned towards the start. In the top part of the course, near the tower, lay a large pond with a couple of swans swimming in stately unison across from two small devoted black and white ducks. Neither pair took the slightest notice of the throng of horses thundering past a few feet from home.

Rinty Ranger won the race, taking the lead at the

beginning of the last circuit and holding off all challengers, and I saw the flash of his triumphant teeth as he went past the post.

The misty daylight had already faded to the limit for jumping fences safely, but the two races still to come, in a card of ten altogether, were both on the flat. The first was run in peering dusk and the second in total darkness, with floodlights from the tower illuminating just the winning line, bright enough to activate the photo-finish. Eleven horses sped up the dark track, clearly seen only for the seconds it took them to flash through the bright patch, but cheered nonetheless by a seemingly undiminished crowd.

So they literally did race in the dark. I walked thoughtfully back towards the officials' room to meet up with Arne. It really had been night-black when Bob Sherman left the racecourse.

There was bustle in the officials' room and a lot of grins and assurances that the takings this day were safe in the safe. Arne reminded several of them that the Chairman had said they could come to the progress-report meeting if they liked: he said it in English in deference to me, and in English they answered. They would come, except for one or two who would wait for the night watchman. A right case of bolting stable doors.

The Chairman's room had too many people in it, as far as I was concerned. Fifteen besides myself. Every chair filled up, coffee and drinks circulated, and the eyes waited. Lars Baltzersen raised his eyebrows in my direction to tell me I was on, and shushed the low-key chatter with a single smooth wave of his hand.

'I think you've all met Mr Cleveland at some time today . . .' He turned directly to me and smiled forgivingly. 'I know we have asked the impossible. Sherman left no traces, no clues. But is there any course of action you think we might take which we have not so far done?'

He made it so easy.

'Look for his body,' I said.

CHAPTER FIVE

It seemed that that was not what they expected.

Per Bjørn Sandvik said explosively in his high, distilled English, 'We know he is a thief. Why should he be dead?' and someone else murmured, 'I still think he is in the south of France, living in the sun.'

Rolf Torp, owner of the Grand National winner, lit a cigar and said, 'I do not follow your reasoning.' Arne sat shaking his head and blinking as if he would never stop.

Lars Baltzersen gave me a slow stare and then invited me to explain.

'Well,' I said. 'Take first the mechanics of that theft. Everyone agrees that the officials' room was empty for a very few minutes, and that no one could have predicted when it would be empty, or that it would be empty at all. Everyone agrees that Bob Sherman simply saw the money lying handy, was overcome with sudden temptation, and swiped it. Sorry...' I said as I saw their puzzlement, '... stole it.'

Heads nodded all round. This was well worn ground.

'After that,' I said, 'we come to a few difficulties. That money was enclosed in five hefty . . . er, bulky . . . canvas bags fastened with straps and padlocks. Now a hundred-and-thirty-three-pound jockey couldn't stow five such bags out of sight under his coat. Anyone, however big, would have found it awkward to pick all of them up at once. To my mind, if Sherman's first impulse was to steal, his second would instantly be to leave well alone. He had no way of knowing how much the bags contained. No way of judging whether the theft would be worthwhile. But in fact there is no evidence at all to suggest that he even felt any impulse to steal, even if he saw the bags on the floor when he went in earlier to ask some question or other. There is no evidence whatsoever to prove that Bob Sherman stole the money.'

'Of course there is,' Rolf Torp said. 'He disappeared.'

'How?' I asked.

There were several puzzled frowns, one or two blank faces, and no suggestions.

'This must have been a spur-of-the-moment theft,' I said, 'so he could have made no preparations. Well, say for argument he had taken the bags, there he is staggering around with the swag . . . the stolen goods . . . in full view. What does he do? Even with a sharp knife it would have taken some time to slit open those bags and remove the money. But we can discount that he did this on the racecourse, because the bags in fact have never been found.'

Some heads nodded. Some were shaken.

'Bob Sherman had a small overnight grip with him, which I understand from his wife was not big enough to contain five canvas bags, let alone his clothes as well. No one has found his clothes lying around, so he could not have packed the money in his grip.'

Lars Baltzersen looked thoughtful.

'Take transport,' I said. 'He had ordered a taxi to take him to Fornebu airport, but he didn't turn up. The police could find no taxi driver who took one single Englishman anywhere. Gunnar Holth says he drove him round to the racecourse at midday, but not away. Because the theft has to be unpremeditated, Sherman could not have hired himself a getaway car, and the police anyway could trace no such hiring. He did not steal a car to transport the money: no cars were stolen from here that day. Which leaves friends . . .' I paused. 'Friends who could be asked to take him say to Sweden, and keep quiet afterwards.'

'They would be also guilty,' said Rolf Torp disbelievingly.

'Yes. Well . . . he had been to Norway seven times but only for a day or two each time. The only friends I can find who might conceivably have known or liked him well enough to get themselves into trouble on his account are Gunnar Holth's head lad, Paddy O'Flaherty, and perhaps . . . if you'll forgive me, sir . . . Mikkel Sandvik.'

He was much more annoyed this time, but protested no further than a grim stare.

'But Paddy O'Flaherty's car has been up on bricks for six weeks,' I said. 'And Mikkel Sandvik cannot drive yet. Neither of them had wheels . . . er, transport . . . ready and waiting for Sherman's unexpected need.'

'What you are saying,' Baltzersen said, 'is that once he'd stolen the money, he couldn't have got it away. But suppose he hid it, and came back for it later?'

'He would still have much the same transport problem, and also the night watchmen to contend with. No . . . I think if he had stolen and hidden the money, he would not have gone back for it, but just abandoned it. Sense would have prevailed. Because there are other things about that cash . . . To you, it is familiar. It is *money*. To Bob Sherman, it was foreign currency. All British jockeys riding abroad have enough trouble changing currency as it is; they would not leap at stealing bagfuls of something they could not readily spend. And don't forget, a large proportion of it was in coins, which are both heavy and even more difficult to exchange in quantity than notes, once they are out of Norway.'

Per Bjørn Sandvik was studying the floor and looking mild again. Arne had blinked his eyes to a standstill and was now holding them shut. Rolf Torp puffed his cigar with agitation and Lars Baltzersen looked unhappy.

'But that still does not explain why you think Sherman is dead,' he said.

'There has been no trace of him from that day to this . . . No one even thinks they might have seen him. There have been no reports from anywhere. His pregnant wife has had no word of reassurance. All this is highly unusual in the case of a thief on the run, but entirely consistent with the man being dead.'

Baltzersen took his bottom lip between his teeth.

I said, 'It is usually fairly easy to account for a man's abrupt disappearance . . . during an investigation his motive emerges pretty strongly. But there seems to have been no factor in Bob Sherman's life likely to prompt him into impulsive and irreversible flight. No one would exchange a successful career for an unknown but not huge amount of foreign currency unless some secondary force made it imperative. Neither your police, nor the British police, nor his wife, nor Arne Kristiansen, nor I, have found any suggestion, however faint or unlikely, that there was such force at work.'

Arne opened his eyes and shook his head.

'Suppose,' I said, 'that someone else stole the money, and Bob Sherman saw him.'

The Stewards and officials looked startled and intensely gloomy. No one needed to have it spelled out that anyone caught red-handed might have had too much to lose, and from there it was a short step to imagine the thief desperate enough to kill Bob Sherman to keep him quiet.

'Murder?' Baltzersen spoke the word slowly as if it were strange on his tongue. 'Is that what you mean?'

'It's possible,' I said.

'But not certain.'

'If there were any clear pointers to murder,' I said, 'your police would have already found them. There is no clarity anywhere. But if there are no answers at all to the questions where he went, why he went, and how he went, I think one should then ask *whether* he went.'

Baltzersen's strained voice mirrored their faces: they did not want me to be right. 'You surely don't think he is still *here*? On the racecourse?'

Rolf Torp shook his head impatiently. He was a man most unlike the Chairman, as quick tempered as Baltzersen was steady. 'Of course he doesn't. There are people here every day training their horses, and we have held eight race meetings since Sherman disappeared. If his body had been here, it would have been found at once.'

Heads nodded in unanimous agreement, and Baltzersen said regretfully, 'I suppose he could have been driven away from here unconscious or dead, and hidden . . . buried . . . later, somewhere else.'

'There's a lot of deep water in Norway,' I said.

My thoughts went back to our little junket in the fjord, and I missed some lightning reaction in someone in that room. I knew that a shift had been made, but because of that gap in concentration I couldn't tell who had made it. Fool, I thought, you got a tug on the line and you didn't see which fish, and even the certainty that a fish was there was no comfort.

The silence lengthened, until finally Per Bjørn Sandvik looked up from the floor with a thoughtful frown. 'It would seem, then, that no one can ever get to the truth of it. I think David's theory is very plausible. It fits all the facts . . . or rather, the lack of facts . . . better than any explanation we have discussed before.'

The heads nodded.

'We will tell our police here what you have suggested,' Baltzersen said in a winding-up-the-meeting voice, 'but I agree with Per . . . After so long a time, and after so much fruitless investigation, we will never really know what happened either to Sherman or to the money. We are all most grateful that you took the trouble to come over, and I know that for most of us, on reflection, your answer to the puzzle will seem the one most likely to be right.'

They gave me a lot of worried half-smiles and some more nods. Rolf Torp stubbed out his cigar vigorously and everyone shifted on their chairs and waited for Baltzersen to stand up.

I thought about the two graceful swans and the two little black and white ducks swimming around quietly out there on the dark side of the tower.

'You could try the pond,' I said.

*

The meeting broke up half an hour later, after it had been agreed with a certain amount of horror that the peaceful little water should be dragged the following morning.

Arne had some security jobs to see to, which he did with painstaking slowness. I wandered aimlessly around, listening to the Norwegian voices of the last of the crowd going home. A good hour after the last race, and still a few lights, still a few people. Not the most private place for committing murder.

I went back towards the weighing room and stood beside the clump of ornamental bushes on the grass outside. Well... they were thick enough and dark enough to have hidden a body temporarily, until everyone had gone. A jockey and his overnight grip, and five bags of stolen money. Plenty of room, in these bushes, for the lot. There were lights outside the weighing room, but the bushes threw heavy shadows and one could not see to their roots.

Arne found me there and exclaimed with passionate certainty, 'He can't be in those, you know. Someone would have seen him long ago.'

'And smelled him,' I said.

Arne made a choking noise and, 'Christ.'

I turned away. 'Have you finished now?'

He nodded, one side of his face brightly lit, the other in shadow. 'The night watchman is here and everything is as it should be. He will make sure all the gates are locked for the night. We can go home.'

79

He drove me in his sturdy Swedish Volvo back towards the city and round to his leafy urban street. Kari greeted us with roaring logs on the fire and tall glasses of frosty thirst-quenching white wine. Arne moved restlessly round the apartment like a bull and switched Beethoven on again, *fortissimo*.

'What's the matter?' Kari asked him, raising her voice. 'For God's sake turn it down.'

Arne obliged, but the sacrifice of his emotional safety valve clearly oppressed him.

'Let him rip,' I told her. 'We can stand it for five minutes.'

Kari gave me a gruesome look and vanished into the kitchen as Arne with great seriousness took me at my word. I sat resignedly on the sofa while the stereophonics shook the foundations, and admired the forebearance of his neighbours. The man who lived alone below my own flat in London had ears like stethoscopes and was up knocking on my door at every dropped pin.

The five minutes stretched to nearly twenty before Arne stopped pacing around and turned down the volume.

'Great stuff, great stuff,' he said.

'Sure,' I agreed because it was, in its place, which was somewhere the size of the Albert Hall.

Kari returned from exile with little wifely indulgent shakes of the head. She looked particularly disturbing in a copper-coloured, silky trouser suit which did fantastic things for the hair, the colouring and the eyes and nothing bad for the rest of her. She refilled our glasses and sat on some floor cushions near the fire.

'How did you enjoy the races?' she asked.

'Very much,' I said.

Arne blinked a bit, said he had some telephone calls to make, and removed himself to the hall. Kari said she had watched the Grand National on television but rarely went to the races herself.

'I'm an indoors person,' she said. 'Arne says the outdoor life is healthier, but I don't enjoy being cold or wet or cut up by the wind, so I let him go off doing all those rugged things like skiing and sailing and swimming, and me, I just make a warm room for him to come back to.'

She grinned, but I caught the faintest of impressions that wifely though she might thoroughly appear to be, she had feelings for Arne which were not wholehearted love. Somewhere deep lay an attitude towards the so-called manly pursuits which was far from admiration; and a basic antipathy to an activity nearly always extended, in my experience, to anyone who went in for it.

Arne's voice floated in from the hall, speaking Norwegian.

'He is talking about dragging a pond,' Kari said, looking puzzled. 'What pond?'

I told her what pond.

'Oh dear ... his poor little wife ... I hope he isn't in there ... how would she bear it?'

Better, I thought, on the whole, than believing he was a thief who had deserted her. I said, 'It's only a possibility. But it's as well to make sure.'

She smiled. 'Arne has a very high opinion of you. I expect you are right. Arne said when he came back from England that he would never want to be investigated by you, you seemed to know what people were thinking. When the Chairman asked for someone to find Bob Sherman and Arne heard that you were coming yourself, he was very pleased. I heard him telling someone on the telephone that you had the eyes of a hawk and a mind like a razor.' She grinned ironically, the soft light gleaming on her teeth. 'Are you flattered?'

'Yes,' I said. 'I wish it were true.'

'It must be true if you are in charge when you are so young.'

'I'm thirty-three,' I said. 'Alexander the Great had conquered the world from Greece to India by that time.'

'You look twenty-five,' she said.

'It's a great drawback.'

'A ... what?'

'A disadvantage.'

'No woman would think so.'

Arne came back from the hall looking preoccupied. 'Everything all right?'

'Oh . . . er . . . *ja*.' He blinked several times. 'It is all arranged. Nine o'clock tomorrow morning, they drag the pond.' He paused. 'Will you be there, David?'

I nodded. 'And you?'

'*Ja*.' The prospect did not seem to please him; but then I was not wildly excited about it myself. If Bob Sherman were indeed there, he would be the sort of unforgettable object you wished you had never seen, and my private gallery of those was already too extensive.

Arne piled logs on the fire as if to ward off demons, and Kari said it was time to eat. She gave us reindeer steaks in a rich dark sauce and after that the promised cloudberries, which turned out to be yellowy-brown and tasted of caramel.

'They are very special,' Arne said, evidently pleased to be able to offer them. 'They grow in the mountains, and are only in season for about three weeks. There is a law about picking them. One can be prosecuted for picking them before the right date.'

'You can get them in tins,' Kari said. 'But they don't taste the same as these.'

We ate in reverent silence.

'No more until next year,' Arne said regretfully, putting down his spoon. 'Let's have some coffee.'

Kari brought the coffee and with amusement declined half-hearted offers from me to help with the dishes.

'You do not want to. Be honest.'

'I do not want to,' I said truthfully.

She laughed. A highly feminine lady with apparently no banners to wave about equality in the kitchen. Between her and Arne the proposition that everything indoors was her domain, and everything outside, his, seemed to lead only to harmony. In my own sister it had led to resentment, rows, and a broken marriage. Kari, it seemed to me, expected less, settled for less, and achieved more.

I didn't stay late. I liked looking at Kari just a shade too much, and Arne, for all his oddnesses, was an investigator. I had taught him myself how to notice where people were looking, because where their eyes were, their thoughts were, as often as not. Some men felt profound gratification when others lusted after their wives, but some felt a revengeful anger. I didn't know what Arne's reaction would be, and I didn't aim to find out.

CHAPTER SIX

Monday morning. Drizzle. Daylight slowly intensifying over Øvrevoll racecourse, changing anthracite clouds to flannel grey. The dark green spruce and yellow birch stood around in their dripping thousands and the paper debris from the day before lay soggily scattered across the wet tarmac.

Round the lower end of the track, Gunnar Holth and one or two other trainers were exercising their strings of racehorses, but the top part, by and above the winning post, had been temporarily railed off.

Shivering from depression more than cold, I was sitting up in the observation tower with Lars Baltzersen, watching the dragging of the pond down below. Hands in pockets, shoulders hunched, rain dripping off hat brims, Arne and two policemen stood at the water's edge, peering morosely at the small boat going slowly, methodically, backwards and forwards from bank to bank.

The pond was more or less round, approximately thirty yards in diameter, and apparently about six feet deep. The boat contained two policemen with grappling hooks and a third, dressed in a black rubber scuba suit, who was doing the rowing. He wore flippers, gloves, hood and goggles, and had twice been over the side with an underwater torch to investigate when the grapples caught. Both times he had returned to the surface and shaken his head.

The swans and the black and white ducks swam around in agitated circles. The water grew muddier and muddier. The boat moved slowly on its tenth traverse, and Lars Baltzersen said gloomily. 'The police think this is a waste of time.'

'Still,' I said, 'they did come.'

'They would, of course.'

'Of course,' I said.

We watched in silence.

A grapple caught. The swimmer went over the side, submerged for a full minute, came up, shook his head, and was helped back into the boat. He took up the oars; rowed on. One each side of the boat, the two men swung the three pronged grapples into the water again, dragging them slowly across the bottom.

'They considered emptying the pond,' Baltzersen said. 'But the technical difficulties are great. Water drains into it from all the top part of the racecourse. They decided on dragging.'

'They are being thorough enough,' I said.

He looked at me soberly. 'If they do not find

Sherman, then, will you be satisfied that he is not there?'

'Yes,' I said.

He nodded. 'That is reasonable.'

We watched for another hour. The swimmer made two more trips into the water, and came up with nothing. The boat finished its journey, having missed not an inch. There was no body. Bob Sherman was not in the pond.

Beside me, Baltzersen stood up stiffly and stretched, his chair scraping loudly on the wooden boards.

'That is all, then,' he said.

'Yes.'

I stood and followed him down the outside staircase, to be met at the bottom by Arne and the policeman in charge.

'No one is there,' he said to me in English, implying by his tone that he wasn't surprised.

'No. But thank you for finding out.'

He, Baltzersen and Arne spoke together for some time in Norwegian, and Baltzersen walked across to thank the boatmen personally. They nodded, smiled, shrugged, and began to load their boat on to a trailer.

'Never mind, David,' said Arne with sympathy. 'It was a good idea.'

'One more theory down the drain,' I agreed philosophically. 'Not the first, by a long way.'

'Will you go on looking?'

I shook my head. The fjords were too deep. Someone

in the Chairman's room had reacted strongly to my mention of water, and if Bob Sherman wasn't in the pond he was somewhere just as wet.

Baltzersen, Arne, the senior policeman and I trudged back across the track and into the paddock enclosure, on our way to the cars parked beside the main entrance. Baltzersen frowned at the rubbish lying around in the shape of dropped race-cards and old tote tickets and said something to Arne. Arne replied in Norwegian and then repeated it in English.

'The manager thought it better that the refuse collectors should not be here to see the police drag the pond. Just in case, you see . . . Anyway, they are coming tomorrow instead.'

Baltzersen nodded. He had taken the morning off from his timber business and looked as though he regretted it.

'I'm sorry,' I said, 'to have wasted your time.'

He made a little movement of his head to acknowledge that I was more or less forgiven. The persistent drizzle put a damper on anything warmer.

In silence we passed the stands, the ornamental pond (too shallow) and secretariat, and it was probably because the only noise was the crunch of our feet that we heard the child.

He was standing in a corner of the Tote building, sobbing. About six, soaked to the skin, with hair plastered to his forehead in forlorn-looking spikes. The policeman looked across to him and beckoned, and in a kind enough voice said what must have been, 'Come here.'

The boy didn't move, but he said something which halted my three companions in mid-step. They stood literally immobile, as if their reflexes had all stopped working. Their faces looked totally blank.

'What did he say?' I asked.

The boy repeated what he had said before, and if anything the shock of my companions deepened.

Baltzersen loosened his jaw with a visible effort, and translated.

'He said, "I have found a hand".'

The child was frightened when we approached, his big eyes looking frantically around for somewhere to run to, but whatever the policeman said reassured him, and when we reached him he was just standing there, wet, terrified, and shivering.

The policeman squatted beside him, and they went into a longish quiet conversation. Eventually the policeman put out his hand, and the child gripped it, and after that the policeman stood up and told us in English what he'd said.

'The boy came to look for money. The racing crowd often drop coins and notes, especially after dark. This boy says he always squeezes through a hole in the fence, before the rubbish collectors come, to see if he can find money. He says he always finds some. This morning he found twenty kroner before the men came. He means before the police came. But he is not supposed to be here, so he hid. He hid behind the stands up there.' The policeman nodded across the tarmac. 'He says that behind the stands he found a hand lying on the ground.'

He looked down at the child clutching his own hand like a lifeline, and asked Arne to go across to his men, who had packed up all their gear and were on the point of leaving, to ask them to come over at the double. Arne gave the child a sick look and did as he was asked, and Baltzersen himself slowly returned to businesslike efficiency.

The policeman had difficulty transferring the boy's trust to one of his men, but finally disengaged himself, and he, two of his men, Baltzersen, Arne and I walked up to and around the stands to see the hand which was lying on the ground.

The child was not mistaken. Waxy white and horrific, it lay back downwards on the tarmac, fingers laxly curled up to meet the rain.

What the child had not said, however, was that the hand was not alone.

In the angle between the wall and the ground lay a long mound covered by a black tarpaulin. Halfway along its length, visible to the wrist, the hand protruded.

Wordlessly the senior policeman took hold of a corner of the tarpaulin and pulled it back.

Arne took one look, bolted for the nearest bushes,

and heaved up whatever Kari had given him for breakfast. Baltzersen turned grey and put a shaking hand over his mouth. The policemen themselves looked sick, and I added another to the unwanted memories.

He was unrecognizable really: it was going to be a teeth job for the inquest. But the height and clothes were right, and his overnight grip was lying there beside him, still with the initials R. T. S. stamped on in black.

A piece of nylon rope was securely knotted round the chest, and another halfway down the legs, and from each knot, one over the breastbone, one over the knees, led a loose piece of rope which finished in a frayed end.

One of the policemen said something to his chief, and Baltzersen obligingly translated for me.

'That is the policeman who was diving,' he said, 'and he says that in the pond the grapples caught on a cement block. He did not think anything of it at the time, but he says there were frayed ends of rope coming from the cement. He says it looked like the same rope as this.'

The policeman in charge pulled the tarpaulin back over the tragic bundle and started giving his men instructions. Arne stood several yards away, mopping his face and mouth with a large white handkerchief and looking anywhere but at the black tarpaulin. I walked over and asked if he was all right. He was trembling, and shook his head miserably.

'You need a drink,' I said. 'You'd better go home.'

'No.' He shuddered. 'I'll be all right. So stupid of me. Sorry, David.'

He came with me round to the front of the stands and we walked over to where Baltzersen and the top policeman had rejoined the little boy. Baltzersen adroitly drew me aside a pace or two, and said quietly, 'I don't want to upset Arne again . . . The child says the hand was not showing at first. He lifted the tarpaulin a little to see what was underneath . . . you know what children are like . . . and he saw something pale and tried to pull it out. It was the hand. When he saw what it was . . . he ran away.'

'Poor little boy,' I said.

'He shouldn't have been here,' he said, meaning by his tone, serve him right.

'If he hadn't been, we wouldn't have found Bob Sherman.'

Lars Baltzersen looked at me thoughtfully. 'I suppose whoever took him out of the pond meant to return with transport and get rid of him somewhere else.'

'No, I shouldn't think so,' I said.

'He must have done. If he didn't mind him being found, he would have left him in the pond.'

'Oh sure. I just meant . . . why take him anywhere else? Why not straight back into the pond . . . as soon as it was dark? That's the one place no one would ever look for Bob Sherman again.'

He gave me a long considering stare, and then unexpectedly, for the first time that morning, he smiled.

'Well . . . you've done what we asked,' he said.

I smiled faintly back and wondered if he yet understood the significance of that morning's work. But catching murderers was a matter for the police, not for me. I was only catching the two-five to Heathrow, with little enough margin for what I still had to do first.

I said, 'Any time I can help . . .' in the idle way that one does, and shook hands with him, and with Arne, and left them there with their problem, in the drizzle.

I picked up Emma Sherman at her hotel as I had arranged, and took her up to my room in the Grand. I had been going to give her lunch before we set off to the airport, but instead I asked the restaurant to bring hot soup upstairs. Still no brandy. Not until three o'clock, they said. Next time, I thought, I'd pack a gallon.

Champagne was emotionally all wrong for the news I had to give her, so I stirred it around with some orange juice and made her drink it first. Then I told her, as gently as I could that Bob had died at the time of his disappearance. I told her he was not a thief and had not deserted her. I told her he had been murdered.

The desperately frail look came back to her face, but she didn't faint.

'You did . . . find him, then.'

'Yes.'

'Where . . . is he?'

'At the racecourse.'

She stood up, swaying a bit. 'I must go and see him.'

'No,' I said firmly, holding her elbow. 'No, Emma, you must not. You must remember him alive. He doesn't look the same now, and he would hate you to see him. He would beg you not to see him.'

'I must see him . . . of course I must.'

I shook my head.

'Do you mean . . .' It began to dawn on her . . . 'That he looks . . . *horrible*?'

'I'm afraid so. He's been dead a month.'

'Oh God.'

She sat down with weak knees and began to cry. I told her about the pond, the ropes, the cement. She had to know some time, and it couldn't be much worse than the agony of spirit she had suffered through four long weeks.

'Oh my poor Bob,' she said. 'Oh darling . . . oh darling . . .'

The floodgates of all that misery were opened and she wept with a fearful outpouring intensity, but at least and at last it was a normal grief, without the self doubt and humiliating shame.

After a while, still shaking with sobs, she said, 'I'll have to get my room back, at the hotel.'

'No,' I said. 'You're coming home to England today, with me, as we planned.'

'But I can't . . .'

'Indeed you can, and indeed you will. The last place for you now is here. You need to go home, to rest, recover, and look after that baby. The police here will do everything necessary, and I'll see that the Jockey Club, and the Injured Jockeys' Fund perhaps, organizes things from the English end. In a little while we can have Bob brought home to England, if that's what you would like . . . But for today, it's you that matters. If you stay here, you will be ill.'

She listened, took in barely half, but in fact raised no more objections. Maybe the police would not be overjoyed at her leaving, I thought, but they'd had her around for a month, and there couldn't be much she hadn't already told them. We caught the flight on schedule, and she stared out of the window all the way home with exhausted tears running intermittently down her cheeks.

Her grandfather, alerted from Oslo, met her at Heathrow. Tall, thin, stooping and kind, he greeted her with a small kiss and many affectionate pats: her parents, she had told me, had died during her school days, leaving her and a brother to be shuttled between relays of other relations. She liked her mother's widowed father best, and wanted him most in her troubles.

He shook my hand.

'I'll see she's looked after,' he said.

He was a nice scholarly man. I gave him my private address and telephone number, in case she needed an inside edge on official help.

CHAPTER SEVEN

Tuesday morning from nine to ten I spent in the office finding out that everyone had been doing just great in my absence and would undoubtedly continue to do so if I disappeared altogether. On my desk lay neat reports of finished inquiries: the man we had suspected of running a retired high-class 'chaser under a hunter's name in a point-to-point had in fact done so and was now in line for a fraud prosecution, and an applicant for a trainer's licence in the Midlands had been found to have totally unsuitable training facilities.

Nothing to make the hair curl. Nothing like weighted bodies in Norwegian ponds.

The whole of the rest of the day was spent with two opposite numbers from the New York Racing Commission who had come to discuss the viability of a world-wide racing investigatory link-up, something along the lines of Interpol. It was one of a series of talks I'd had with officials of many countries and the idea seemed very slowly to be staggering towards achievement. As usual the chief stumbling block to any rapid progress seemed to be my own apparent youth: I supposed that by the time I was sixty, when I'd run out of steam, they would begin to nod while they listened.

I talked my throat dry, gave away sheaves of persuasive literature, took them to dinner at Inigo Jones, and hoped the seed hadn't fallen on stony ground. At farewell time the older of them asked a question I was by then well used to.

'If you succeed in setting this thing up, do you have it in mind to be head of it yourself?'

I smiled. I knew very well that if the baby was born it would very smartly be found to be not mine after all.

'Once it's set up,' I said, 'I'll move on.'

He looked at me curiously.

'Where to?'

'Don't know yet.'

They shook their heads and tut-tutted slightly, but gripped hands with cordiality as we separated into a couple of homeward taxis. It was after midnight when I reached the house where I lived behind the Brompton Road, but as usual the lights were still on in the rooms below my own small flat. The street door banged if you let it go, reverberating through the walls, and perhaps that, I thought, as I shut it gently, explained the ground floor tenant's hypersensitivity. He was a self-contained man, greyish, fiftyish, very neat and precise. Our acquaintanceship after six months of living stacked one over the other extended simply to his trips to my door urging an instant lessening of decibels on the television. Once I had asked him in for a drink, but he politely declined, preferring solitude downstairs. Hardly the *entente cordiale* of the century.

I went up, opened my own door, and shut that quietly also. The telephone bell, starting suddenly in all that noble silence, made me jump.

'Mr Cleveland?' The voice was hurried, practically incoherent. 'Thank goodness you're back at last . . . This is William Romney . . . Emma's grandfather . . . She didn't want me to ring you so late, but I must . . . Two men were searching her house when she went in and they hit her . . . Mr Cleveland . . . she needs your help . . .'

'Stop a minute,' I said. 'First thing you need is the police.'

He calmed down a fraction. 'They've been here. Just left. I called them.'

'And a doctor for Emma?'

'Yes, yes. He's gone, too.'

'What time did all this happen?'

'About seven this evening . . . we drove over from my house just to fetch some things for her . . . and there was a light on . . . and she went in first and they jumped on her . . . they hit us both . . . I do wish . . . well . . . tell you the truth . . . I think we're both still frightened.'

I stifled a sigh. 'Where exactly are you?'

'At Emma's house, still.'

'Yes, but . . .'

99

'Oh, I see. Near Newbury. You go down the M4...'
He gave me details of the journey, certain in his own
mind that I would hurry to their aid. He made it
impossible for me to say take a tranquillizer and I'll
come in the morning, and anyway, by the sound of his
voice, nothing short of a full anaesthetic was going to
give him any rest.

At least at night it was a fast straightforward journey,
so I took the MGB down there in fifty minutes flat.
The Shermans' house proved to be a modernized pair
of farm cottages down an uninhabited lane, a nerve-
testing isolation at the best of times.

Lights were on in every window, and at the sound
of my car William Romney's anxious figure appeared
in the doorway.

'Thank goodness, thank goodness,' he said agitatedly,
coming down the short path to meet me. 'I don't know
what we would have done... if you hadn't been
coming...'

I refrained from saying that I thought they should
have gone back to his house or otherwise stayed in a
hotel, and once through the door I was glad I hadn't,
because it wouldn't have helped. Shock prevents people
from leaving the scene of personal disaster of their own
accord, and of the scope and depth of their shock there
could be no doubt.

The house was a shambles. Pictures had been torn
from the walls, curtains from the windows, carpets from the
floor. Furniture was not merely turned inside out, but

smashed. Lamps, vases, ornaments lay in pieces. Papers and books scattered the wreckage like autumn leaves.

'It's all like this,' Romney said. 'The whole house. All except the spare bedroom. That's where they were when we interrupted them. The police say so . . .'

Emma herself was in the spare bedroom, lying awake with eyes like soot smudges. Both of her cheeks were swollen and puffy, with red marks showing where blows had landed. Her lower lip had been split, and one eyebrow ended in a raw skinned patch.

'Hullo,' I said inadequately, and pulled up a chair so that I could sit beside her. Her grandfather hovered around making fussing noises, obviously freshly worried by the darkening bruises but tiring Emma beyond bearing. He looked more upset than ever when I asked him if I could speak to her alone, but in the end he reluctantly returned to the devastation below.

I held her hand.

'David . . .'

'Wait a bit,' I said. 'Then tell me.'

She nodded slightly. She was lying on the blankets of the unmade bed, still wearing the brown and white checked dress, her head supported by two coverless pillows and with a flowered quilt over her from the waist down.

The room was hot with a pulsating gas fire, but Emma's hand was cold.

'I told the police,' she said, 'I think they were Norwegians.'

'The two men?'

She nodded. 'They were big... They had thick sweaters and rubber gloves... They talked with accents...'

'Start at the beginning,' I said.

She loosened her mouth, obviously troubled by the split and swelling lip.

'We came over to get me some different clothes. I was beginning to feel better... There was a light on upstairs but I thought Mrs Street who has been looking after the house had left it on... but when I unlocked the front door and went into the hall they jumped on me... they switched all the lights on... I saw the mess... One of them hit me in the face and I screamed for Grandad... When he came in they knocked him over... so easily, it was awful... and they kicked him... One of them asked me where Bob would hide papers... and when I didn't answer at once he just went on... punching me in the face... with his fists... I didn't answer because I didn't know... Bob doesn't hide things... didn't... oh God...'

Her fingers curled tight round mine.

'All right, all right, Emma,' I said, meaning nothing except that I understood. 'Wait a bit.'

We waited until some of the tension left her body; then she swallowed and tried again.

'The telephone rang then, and it seemed to worry them. They talked to each other, and then suddenly they just threw me into a chair... and they went away . . . through the front door . . . Grandad got up off the floor but the telephone stopped before he reached it . . . but anyway he called the police . . .'

The tired voice stopped. I said, 'Did the men wear masks of any sort?'

'No.'

'Would you know them again?'

'The police asked . . . they want me to look at photographs . . . but I don't know . . . I was trying to avoid being hurt . . . I tried to put my hands in front of my face . . . and I shut my eyes . . .'

'How about your grandfather?'

'He says he might know them . . . but it was over so quickly, really.'

'I suppose they didn't tell you what papers they were looking for?'

She shook her head miserably. 'The police asked me that, over and over.'

'Never mind,' I said. 'How does your face feel now?'

'Awfully stiff. Dr West gave me some pills, though. He says he'll look in again tomorrow.'

'Here?'

'Yes . . . I didn't want to go back to Grandad's. This . . . this is . . . home.'

'Do you want the bed made properly?'

'No thank you. I'm comfortable like this . . . too tired to move.'

'I'll go down, then, and give your grandfather a hand.'

'All right . . .' Anxiety flooded her suddenly. 'But you won't go, will you?'

I promised her, and in fact I slept in trousers and shirt on the sofa in the sitting-room on a cleared oasis amid the rubble. William Romney, taxed almost too far, snored gently with a strong sedative on the double bed in the Shermans' own room, and from three o'clock to five the cottage was dark and quiet.

I awoke suddenly with a soft wail in my ears like the sound of a lamb in a snowstorm.

'David . . .'

It was Emma's voice from upstairs, urgent and quavery.

I tossed off the rug, stood up, and beat it up there fast. I'd left her door open and the fire on, and as I went in I could see the ultimate disaster looking out of her great dark eyes.

'David . . .' Her voice filled with inconsolable desolation. 'David . . . I'm bleeding.'

She lost the baby and very nearly her life. I went to see her three days after she'd been whisked away in a bell-ringing ambulance (three days because no one was allowed in sooner) and was surprised to discover that she could and did look even paler than she had in Oslo. The swellings had gone down in her face, though the bruises showed dark in patches. Her eyes were dulled, which seemed a mercy.

The five minutes visit passed on the surface.

'Nice of you to come,' she said.

'Brought you some grapes.'

'Very kind.'

'Sorry about the baby.'

She nodded vaguely, but some sort of drug was dealing with that pain also.

'Hope you'll soon be better.'

'Oh yes. Yes, I will.'

William Romney shook with fury, stamping up and down my office with outrage.

'Do you realize that it is a week tomorrow since we were attacked and no one has done *anything*? People can't just vanish into thin air ... those men must be somewhere ... why can't the police find them? It isn't right that thugs should just walk into a defenceless girl's house and tear things to pieces and hurt her so much that she nearly dies of it ... It's *disgraceful* that the police haven't found those despicable *bastards* ...'

The word was a strong one for him: he looked almost surprised that he'd used it, and nothing could have more clearly stated the fierceness of his feelings.

'I believe neither you nor Emma could identify the men from police photographs,' I said, having checked via a friendly police contact that this was so.

'They weren't there. There weren't any pictures of them. Can't say that's surprising ... why don't the police get photographs of *Norwegian* crooks for us to look at?'

'It would probably mean your going to Norway,' I said. 'And Emma's in no state, physical or emotional, to do that.'

'I'll go then,' he said belligerently. 'I'll go, at my own expense. Anything . . . *anything* to see those men punished for what they've done to Emma.'

His thin face was flushed with the strength of his resentment. I wondered if part of his fury sprang from unnecessary guilt that he hadn't been young and strong enough to defend or rescue her from two aggressive toughs. Amends in the shape of effort and expense were what he was offering, and I saw no reason to dissuade him from a journey which would bring him mental ease even if no concretely helpful results.

'I'll fix it for you, if you like,' I said.

'What . . .?'

'To go to Norway and look at the mug-shots.'

His resolution took shape and hardened. He straightened his stooping shoulders, calmed his voice, and stopped wearing out so much of the Jockey Club's carpet.

'Yes. Please do that. I'll go as soon as I can.'

I nodded. 'Sit down,' I said. 'Do you smoke? And how's Emma?'

He sat down, declined a desk-box of cigarettes, and said that last evening, when he'd seen her, Emma was very much stronger.

'She says she'll be out of hospital in two or three days.'

'Good.'

He didn't look as if it were good. He said in recurring worried anger, 'What on earth is that poor girl going to do? Her husband murdered . . . her home wrecked . . . I suppose she can live with me, but . . .'

'I'm sure she'll live in her own house,' I said. 'For a while, at least. Best if she does. Get her grieving done properly.'

'What an extraordinary thing to say.'

'When can you go?' I said, reaching for the telephone.

'At once.'

'Right.'

Øvrevoll racecourse answered in the shape of the manager who gave me the home and office telephone numbers of Lars Baltzersen. He answered from his office, and I explained the situation. Of course, he said in dismay, of course he could arrange it with the police. For tomorrow? Certainly. Poor Mrs Sherman, he said, please give her my condolences. I said I would, and asked if there had been any recent progress.

'None at all, I'm afraid,' he said. He hesitated for several seconds, and then went on, 'I have been thinking . . . I suppose . . . if the police don't solve this crime . . . that you wouldn't come back yourself, and see what you can do?'

I said, 'I'm not experienced in murder investigation.'

'It must in essence be the same as any other sort.'

'Mm . . . My masters here might not be willing for me to take the time.'

'If I asked them myself, as an international favour? After all, Bob Sherman was a British jockey.'

'Wouldn't Norway prefer to ship him home and forget about the whole nasty incident?'

'No, Mr Cleveland,' he said severely. 'A murder has been done, and justice should follow.'

'I agree.'

'Then . . . you'll come?'

I thought. 'Wait another week. Then if neither your police nor ours have found any new leads, and if you still want me to, well, maybe I can. But . . . don't expect too much, will you?'

'No more than before,' he said dryly, and disconnected.

William Romney had adjusted by then to the prospect of travelling the next day, and began to fuss mildly about tickets, currency and hotels. I shooed him out because he could do all that for himself, and I had a good deal of work on hand to start with, and more still if I had to clear time for another trip to Oslo. The police, I hoped, would quickly dig down to the roots themselves and save me from proving to the world that I couldn't.

*

William Romney went to Norway, spent two full days there and returned depressed. The Norwegian police did not have photographs of the intruders, or if they did, Romney did not recognize them.

Emma left hospital and went home to put her house straight. An offer from me to help her do that was declined; one to come down and take her out to lunch was accepted.

'Sunday?' I suggested.

'Fine.'

Sunday found the carpets flat on the floors, the pictures back on the walls, the broken mess cleared away, and the curtains bundled up for the cleaners. The house looked stark and unlived-in, but its mistress had come a long way back to life. For the first time since I had known her, she was wearing lipstick. Her hair was newly washed, her clothes neat, her manner composed. The pretty girl lurked not far away now, just below the still over-pale skin, just behind the still unhappy eyes.

'It's his funeral on Thursday,' she said.

'Here?'

She nodded. 'In the church in the village. Thank you for doing everything about bringing him home.'

I had delegated the whole job. 'I only got it done,' I said.

'Anyway . . . thanks.'

The October day was calm and sunny and crisp round the edges. I took her to a Thames-side pub where pointed yellow willow leaves floated slowly past on grey water and anglers flicked maggots on hooks to wily fish. We walked along the bank; slowly, because she was still weak from haemorrhage.

'Have you any plans?' I asked.

'I don't know . . . I've thought a lot, of course, while I've been in hospital. I'll go on living in the cottage for a while, I think. It feels right, somehow. In the end I suppose I'll sell it, but not yet.'

'How are the finances?'

She produced a flicker of smile. 'Everyone is being fantastic. Really marvellous. Did you know, the owners Bob rode for in Norway clubbed together and sent me a cheque? How kind people are.'

Conscience money, I thought sourly, but I didn't say so.

'Those two men who burst into your house, do you mind if we talk about them?'

She sighed. 'I don't mind.'

'Describe them.'

'But . . .'

'Yes, I've read what you told the police. You didn't look at them, you shut your eyes, you only saw their sweaters and their rubber gloves.'

'That's right.'

'No. What you told the police was all you could bear to remember, and you would have shut out even that if they hadn't pressed you for answers.'

'That's nonsense.'

'Try it another way. Which one hit you?'

She said instantly, 'The bigger one with the . . .' Her voice stopped uncertainly.

'With the what?'

'I was going to say, with the reddish hair. How odd. I didn't remember until now that one of them had reddish hair.'

'What about the other?'

'Brown. Brown hair. He was kicking Grandad.'

'The one who was hitting you . . . what was he saying?'

' "Where does your husband keep secret papers? Where does he hide things? Tell us where he hides things." '

'Good English?'

'Ye-es. Pretty good. He had an accent.'

'What were his eyes like, while he was hitting you?'

'Fierce . . . frightful . . . like an eagle . . . sort of black and yellow . . . very angry.'

There was a small silence, then she said, 'Yes, I do remember, like you said. I shut it out.'

After a few seconds, 'He was quite young, about the same as you. His mouth was very tight . . . his lips were stiff . . . his face looked hard . . . very angry.'

'How tall?'

'Same as you, about. Broader, though. Much heavier. Big thick shoulders.'

'Big shoulders in a thick sweater. What sort of thick sweater? Did it have a pattern?'

'Well, yes, that was why . . .' She stopped again.

'Why what?'

'Why I thought at once that he was Norwegian . . . before he even spoke. Because of the patterns in his sweater. They were sort of white patterns . . . two colours, though, I think . . . all over a brown sweater. I'd seen dozens like it in the shops in Oslo.' She looked puzzled. 'Why didn't I think of that before?'

'Memories often work like that. Sort of delayed action.'

She smiled. 'I must say it's easier remembering things quietly here by the river than in all that mess with my face hurting and policemen asking me questions from all sides and bustling about . . .'

We went indoors for a drink and a good lunch, and over coffee I asked her other things.

'You said Bob never hid papers. Are you sure?'

'Oh yes. He wasn't secretive. Never. He was more careless, really, than anything else, when it came to papers and documents and things like that.'

'It seems quite extraordinary that two men should come all the way from Norway to search your house for papers.'

She frowned. 'Yes, it does.'

'And to search it so violently, so destructively, so thoroughly.'

'And they were so angry, too.'

'Angry, I expect, because they'd worked hard and hadn't found what they'd come for.'

'But what *did* they come for?'

'Well...' I said slowly. 'Something to do with Norway. What papers did Bob ever have that had anything to do with Norway?'

She shook her head. 'Nothing much. A few receipts, for the accounts. Race-cards, sometimes. A cutting from a Norwegian paper with a picture of him winning a race. Nothing, honestly, that anyone could want.'

I drank my coffee, considering. I said, 'Look at it the other way round... Did he ever take any papers *to* Norway?'

'No. Why should he?'

'I don't know. I just wondered. Because those men might have been looking for something he hadn't taken to Norway, not for something he had brought away.'

'You do think some weird things.'

'Mm...'

I paid the bill and drove her home. She was silent most of the way, but thoughtful, and the fruit of that was a plum.

'I suppose...well, it's stupid, really...but it couldn't have anything to do with blue pictures?'

'What sort of blue pictures?' I asked.

'I don't know. I didn't see them. Only Bob said that's what they were.'

I pulled up outside her gate but made no move to leave the car.

'Did he get them in Norway?'

She was surprised. 'Oh no. It was like you said. He was taking them over there with him. In a brown

113

envelope. It came by hand the night before he went. He said they were blue pictures which a chap in Oslo wanted him to bring over.'

'Did he say what chap?'

She shook her head. 'No. I hardly listened. I'd forgotten all about it until you said . . .'

'Did you see the brown envelope? How big was it?'

'I must have seen it. I mean, I know it was brown.' She frowned, concentrating. 'Fairly big. Not an ordinary letter. About the size of a magazine.'

'Was it marked "photographs", or anything like that?'

'I don't think so. I can't remember. It's more than six weeks ago.' Her eyes filled suddenly with tears. 'He put it in his overnight grip at once, so as not to forget to take it.' She sniffed twice, and found a handkerchief. 'So he did take it to Norway. It wasn't in the house for those men to find. If that's what they were looking for . . . they did all that for nothing.' She put the handkerchief to her mouth and stifled a sob.

'Was Bob interested in blue pictures?' I asked.

'Like any other man, I suppose,' she said through the handkerchief. 'He'd look at them.'

'But he wouldn't collect them himself?'

She shook her head.

I got out of the car, opened the door her side, and went with her into the cottage. She looked at the racing pictures of Bob which hung in the hall.

'They tore all those photographs out of the frames,' she said. 'Some of them were ruined.'

Many of the prints were about ten inches by eight. A magazine-sized brown envelope would have held them easily.

I stayed another hour simply to keep her company, but for the evening ahead she insisted that she would be all right alone. She looked round the bareness of the sitting-room and smiled to herself. She obviously found the place friendly, and maybe Bob was there too.

When I went she gave me a warm kiss on the cheek and said, 'I can't thank you enough . . .' and then broke off and opened her eyes wide.

'Golly,' she said. 'That was the second lot.'

'What of?'

'Blue pictures. He took some before. Oh . . . months ago. Back in the summer.' She shook her head in fresh frustration. 'I can't remember. I just remember him saying . . . blue pictures.'

I kissed her in return.

'Take care of yourself,' I said.

'You, too.'

CHAPTER EIGHT

A little matter of doping-to-win took me to Plumpton races in Sussex the following day but I saw no harm in some extra spadework on the side. Rinty Ranger, busy in second and fifth races, was comparatively easy to pin down between the third and the fourth.

'What did you say?' he repeated in exaggerated amazement. 'Take pornography to Scandinavia? Christ, that's like wasting pity on bookmakers. They don't need it, mate. They don't bloody need it.'

'Bob Sherman told his wife he was taking blue pictures to Norway.'

'And she believed it?'

'The point is, did he?'

'He never said a word about it to me.'

'Do me a favour,' I said. 'Find out in the changing-room here today if anyone ever asked any jockey to act as a messenger ... a carrier ... of any papers of any sort from Britain to Norway.'

'Are you serious?'

'Bob Sherman's dead.'

116

'Yes.' He thought. 'OK.'

He gave me a noncommittal wave as he walked out to the fifth, in which he rode a bright, tight, tactical race to be beaten half a length by a better horse, but came straight out of the weighing room after he had changed and put an end to my easy theory.

'None of them who have ridden in Norway has ever been asked to take over any papers or pictures or anything like that.'

'Would they say, if they had?'

He grinned. 'Depends how much they'd been paid to forget.'

'What do you think yourself?'

'Hard to tell. But they all seemed surprised. There weren't any knowing looks, sort of, if you see what I mean.'

'Carry on asking, would you? Tomorrow and so on. Say they can tell me hush hush, if they like. No kick backs if they've been fiddling currency.'

He grinned again. 'Some copper you are. Bend the rules like curling tongs.'

That evening I telephoned Baltzersen at his home. There was no news, he said. He had consulted his friends in the police, and they would raise no objections if I joined the hunt. On the contrary, they would, as before, let me see what they'd got, to save me reploughing their furrows.

'So, Mr Cleveland, will you come?'

'I guess so,' I said.

With flattering relief he said, 'Good, good,' explosively, and added, 'come tomorrow.'

''Fraid I can't. I have to give evidence in court tomorrow, and the case may last two days. Soonest would be Thursday morning.'

'Come straight to the racecourse then. We have a meeting on Thursday and another on Sunday, but I fear they may be the last this year. It's a little colder now, and we have had frost.'

I wrote 'warm clothes' in large letters on my memo pad and said I'd see him at the races.

'By the way,' I said. 'You know I told you the people who broke into the Shermans' house were looking for papers? Mrs Sherman now remembers that Bob took with him to Norway a packet which had been entrusted to him, which he believed contained blue pictures. Did anyone mention to you, or to the police, or to Arne in all those preliminary investigations into his disappearance, anything at all about his bringing such a packet with him, or delivering it?'

There was an unexpectedly long silence on the other end of the line, but in the end he only said uncertainly, 'Blue pictures . . . what are those?'

'Pornography.'

'I see.' Another pause. 'Please explain a little.'

I said, 'If the package reached its destination, then it cannot be that particular package that the men were searching for. So I could stop chasing after innocent blue pictures and start looking elsewhere.'

'*Ja*. I see.' He cleared his throat. 'I haven't heard of any such package, but perhaps Arne or the police have done. I will ask them. Of course you know it is unlikely that anyone would need to bring pornography secretly into this country?'

'It would have to be special,' I said, and left it at that.

All Tuesday and Wednesday morning I spent in court giving evidence for the prosecution in an insurance swindle involving grievous cruelty to horses, and Wednesday afternoon I sat in the office juggling six jobs at once like some multi-armed Siva. Looking for Bob Sherman's murderer had meant advancing myself a week's leave when I was too busy to take one, and by seven o'clock when I locked up and left, I was wishing he'd got himself bumped off at any other time.

I went home on tube and feet, thinking comforting thoughts about a large scotch indoors followed by a stroll round to a local grill for a steak. I shut the street door without letting it bang, put one foot in front of the other up the carpeted stairs, unlocked the door to my own flat and switched on the lights; and it was at that point that the day stopped operating according to schedule.

I heard, felt, maybe assimilated by instinct, a change

119

in the air behind me. Nothing as definite as a noise. More a current. Undoubtedly a threat.

All those useful dormant jungle reactions came to my rescue before a thought process based on reason had time to get off the ground. So I was already whipping round to face the stairs and pushing further through my own doorway when the man with the knife did his best to send me early to the cemetery.

He did not have reddish hair, angry yellow eagle eyes or a Norwegian sweater. He did have rubber gloves, a stocky muscular body, a lot of determination and a very sharp blade.

The stab which had been supposed to stop my heart from the back ripped instead through some decent Irish tweed, through a blue cotton shirt below that, and down half a dozen inches of skin on my chest.

He was surprised and fed up that at first he hadn't succeeded, but he'd heard all about try try again. He crowded through my door after me with the knife already rising for another go. I backed through the tiny hall and into the sitting-room, unable to take my eyes off his intentions long enough to find any household object to fight him off with.

He came on with a feint and a slice at my middle regions and I got another rip in my jacket and a closer look at some narrowed and murderous eyes.

He tried next a sort of lunging jump, the point of the knife coming in fast and upward. I tried to leap away backwards, tripped on a rug, fell on my back and found my hand hitting the base of the standard lamp. One wild clutch and I'd pulled it over, knocking him off his aim just when he thought he finally had me. The lamp hit him with a crash and while he was off balance I got both my hands on his knife arm; but it was then that I discovered the rock-like muscles. And also, unfortunately, that he was more or less ambidexterous.

He shifted the knife like lightning from his right hand to his left and I avoided the resulting stab only by a sort of swinging jump over an armchair, using his arm as a lever. The blade hit a cushion and feathers floated up like snowflakes.

I threw a cigarette box at him and missed, and after that a vase which hit but made no difference. As long as I kept the armchair between us he couldn't reach me, but neither did he give me much chance of getting past him to the still open door to the stairs.

Behind me on a wide shelf stood my portable television. I supposed it might stop him if I threw it at him, but on the other hand . . . I stretched out backwards without losing sight of his knife, found the on-off switch, and turned the volume up to maximum.

The din when it started took him totally by surprise and gave me a fractional chance. I pushed the armchair viciously forward at his knees and he overbalanced, twisting as he tried to get his feet under him. He went down as far as one knee, partially recovered, and toppled altogether when I shoved again with the chair. But it was nothing permanent. He was rolling back to his feet like a cat before I had time to get round the big chair and step on some of his tender bits.

Up until that point he had said not a word and now if he did I wouldn't hear: the television literally vibrated with the intense noise of some pop star or other's Special Spectacular; and if that didn't bring the US cavalry, nothing would.

He came. Looking cross. Ready to blow like a geyser. And stood there in consternation in my open door.

'Fetch the police,' I yelled, but he didn't hear. I slapped the off switch.

'Fetch the police,' I yelled again, and my voice bounced off the walls in the sudden silence.

The man with the knife turned to see, gave himself fresh instructions, and went for my friend from downstairs. I did a sort of sliding rugger tackle, throwing myself feet first at his legs. He stumbled over my shoes and ankles and went down on his side. I swept one leg in an arc and by sheer good luck kicked him on the wrist. The knife flew out of his hand at least ten feet, and fell nearer to me than him, and only at that point did he think of giving up.

He scrambled to his feet, looked at me with the first sign of uncertainty, then made up his mind, turned on his heel, crashed past my neighbour and jumped down the stairs in two giant strides. The front door slammed behind him with a force that shook the building, and from the window I saw him running like the Olympics under the street lamps.

I looked breathlessly at the mess in my sitting-room and at my man from downstairs.

'Thanks,' I said.

He took a tentative step into the sitting-room.

'You're bleeding,' he said.

'But not dying.'

I picked up the standard lamp.

'Was he a burglar?' he asked.

'A murderer,' I said. 'Enter a murderer.'

We looked at each other in what was no doubt professional curiosity on both sides, because all he said next was, 'Sit down, you're suffering from shock.'

It was advice I'd given pretty often to others, and it made me smile. All the same there was a perceptible tremble somewhere around my knees, so I did as he said.

He looked around the room, looked at the knife still lying where it had fallen, and took it all in quietly.

'Shall I carry out your instructions, or were they principally a diversion?'

'Hm?'

'Fetch the police.'

'Oh . . . It can wait a bit.'

He nodded, considered a moment, and then said, 'If you'll excuse me asking, why was he trying to kill you?'

'He didn't say.'

My neighbour's name was Stirling. C. V. Stirling, according to the neat white card beside his bell push. He had grey patches neatly brushed back over his ears and nostrils pinched into an expression of distaste for bad smells. His hands looked excessively clean and well manicured, and even in these bizarre circumstances he wore a faint air of exasperated patience. A man used to being the brightest person around, I guessed, with the power to make it felt.

'Did he need to?'

'It would have been helpful,' I said.

He came a pace nearer.

'I could do something about that bleeding, if you like.'

I looked down at the front of my shirt, which had changed colour pretty thoroughly from blue to red.

'Could you?'

'I'm a surgeon,' he said. 'Ear, nose and throat, actually. Other areas by arrangement.'

I laughed. 'Stitch away, then.'

He nodded, departed downstairs, and returned with a neat flat case containing the tools of his trade. He used clips not needles. The slice through my skin was more gory than deep, bleeding away persistently like a shaving nick. When he'd finished, it was a thin red line under a sticking plaster.

'You were lucky,' he said.

'Yes, I was.'

'Do you do this sort of thing often? Fight for your life, I mean.'

'Very rarely.'

'My fee for professional services rendered is a little more chat.'

I smiled wryly.

'OK. I'm an investigator. I don't know why I was attacked unless there's someone around who particularly does not want to be investigated.'

'Good God.' He stared at me curiously. 'A private eye? Philip Marlowe, and all that?'

'Nothing so fancy. I work in racing; for the Jockey Club. Looking into small frauds, most of the time.'

'This,' he waved at my chest and the knife and the scattered cushion feathers, 'doesn't look like a small fraud.'

It didn't. It didn't look, either, even like a severe warning off. It looked like a ruthless all-out push for a final solution.

I changed my clothes and took him round to the grill for the overdue steak. His name was Charles, he said, and we walked home as friends. When I let myself in upstairs and reviewed the general untidiness it occurred to me that in the end I had never called in the police. It seemed a little late to bother, so I didn't.

CHAPTER NINE

I caught the eleven twenty-five to Norway the next morning with the knife wrapped in polythene in my sponge-bag; or rather the black, zipped-leather case which did that duty. It was a hunter's knife, the sort of double-sided blade used for skinning and disjointing game. The cutting edges had been sharpened like razors and the point would have been good as a needle. A professional job: no amateur could have produced that result with a few passes over a carborundum.

The handle was of horn of some sort, but workman-like not tourist-trap stuff. Between handle and blade protruded a short silver bar for extra leverage with fingers. There were no fingerprints on it anywhere, and no blood. Punched into the blade near the hilt were the words *Norsk Stål*.

Its owner hadn't, of course, intended to leave it behind. Just one dead body neatly disposed inside its own front door, out of sight and undiscovered for a minimum of twenty-four hours.

He hadn't followed me into the house: he'd been

there before I came, waiting higher up the stairs for me to come home.

At breakfast time I'd knocked on the doors of the other three tenants, the one in the basement, the one above me, and the one above that, and asked them if they'd seen my visitor on the stairs or let him in through the front door. I got negatives all round, but as one of them said, we were hardly a matey lot, and if the visitor entered boldly while one of the tenants was leaving, no one would have stopped him. None of them remembered him, but the basement man observed that as the laundry van had called that day, a stranger could easily have walked in with the man who collected and delivered the boxes from the hall.

There had been nothing suspicious or memorable about my visitor's appearance. His face was a face; hair brown, skin sallow, eyes dark. Age, about thirty. Clothes, dark grey trousers, navy close-fitting sweater, neat shirt and tie showing at the neck. Entirely the right rig for the neighbourhood. Even a little formal.

BEA landed on time at Fornebu and I took a taxi straight out to the racecourse. Nothing much had changed in the two and a half weeks I'd been away, not even the weather or the runners in the races, and within the first half hour I had spotted all the same faces, among them Gunnar Holth, Paddy O'Flaherty, Per Bjørn Sandvik, Rolf Torp and Lars Baltzersen. Arne greeted me with a beaming smile and an invitation to spend as much time with Kari and himself as I could.

I walked around with him for most of the afternoon, partly from choice, partly because Baltzersen was busy being Chairman. Arne said that whereas he personally was pleased to see me, many of the racecourse committee had opposed Baltzersen in the matter of bringing me back.

'Lars told us at the Tuesday committee meeting that you were definitely coming today, and that caused quite a row. You should have heard it. Lars said that the racecourse would be paying your fare and expenses like last time, and half of them said it was unjustifiable to spend so much.'

He broke off rather suddenly as if he had decided not to repeat what had actually been said.

'I could easily have been persuaded to stay at home,' I said. But by words, I reflected. Not knives.

'Several of the committee said Lars had no right to act without taking a vote.'

'And Lars?'

Arne shrugged. 'He wants Bob Sherman's death explained. Most of them just want to forget.'

'And you?' I asked.

He blinked. 'Well,' he said, 'I would give up more easily than Lars or you. Which is no doubt why,' he grinned, 'Lars is Chairman and you are the chief invest-igator, and I am only a security officer who lets the racecourse takings be stolen from under his nose.'

I smiled. 'No one blames you.'

'Perhaps they should.'

I thought in my intolerant way that they definitely should, but I shook my head and changed the subject.

'Did Lars tell you all about the attack on Emma Sherman, and about her losing her baby?'

'Yes,' he said. 'Poor girl.' There was more lip-service in his voice than genuine regret. I supposed that no one who hadn't seen her as I had could properly understand all that she'd suffered; and I knew that it was in great part because of Emma that I was back in Norway. No one should be allowed to inflict such hurt on another human being, and get away with it. The fact that the same agency had murdered Bob and tried to see me off was in a curious way secondary: it was possible future victims who had to be saved. If you don't dig ground elder out of the flower beds it can strangle the garden.

Rolf Torp was striding about in a bad temper. His horse, he said, had knocked itself that morning and his trainer had omitted to tell him it couldn't run. He had taken the afternoon off from his mining office, which he wouldn't have done if he'd known, on account of being indispensable and nothing constructive ever being achieved in his absence.

After he had delivered himself of that little lot he adjusted his sights more specifically on me.

'I was against bringing you back. I'll tell you that myself. I told the committee. It is a waste of our money.'

His name was on the list Emma had given me of the contributors to the solidly worthwhile cheque the Norwegian owners had sent. If he thought that any available cash should only be spent on the living, perhaps it was a valid point of view; but he wasn't paying my expenses out of his own private pocket.

He was a man of less than average height and more than average aggressiveness: a little bull of a man with a large black moustache that was more a statement than an adornment. Difficult to please and difficult to like, I thought, but sharp of eye and brain as well as tongue.

His voice boomed as heavily as a bittern in the reed beds, and although his English was as comprehensive as most well-educated Norwegians', he spoke it unlovingly, as if he didn't care too much for the taste.

I said without heat, 'As a miner, you'll understand that surveys are a legitimate expense even when they don't strike ore.'

He gave me a hard look. 'As a miner I understand that I would not finance a survey to find slime.'

Klonk. One over the head for D. Cleveland. I grinned appreciatively, and slowly, unwillingly, the corners of his mouth twitched.

I made the most of it. 'May I come and see you in your office?' I asked. 'Just for a few questions. I might as well try my best to earn what you're paying me, now that I'm here.'

'Nothing I can tell you will be of any help,' he said, as if believing made it so.

'Still . . .'

The vestiges of smile disappeared, but finally, grudgingly, he nodded.

'Very well. Tomorrow afternoon. Four o'clock.' And he went so far as to tell me how to find him.

As he walked away Arne said, 'What are you going to ask him?'

'Don't know yet. I just want to see his background. You can't tell what people are really like if you only meet them at the races.'

'But,' he said, blinking furiously, 'why Rolf Torp?'

'Not especially Rolf Torp,' I said. 'Everyone who knew Bob Sherman.'

'David!' He looked staggered. 'It will take you months.'

I shook my head. 'Several days, that's all. Bob didn't know so many people here as all that.'

'But he could have been killed by a total stranger. I mean, if he saw someone stealing the money and didn't know him . . .'

'It's possible,' I said, and asked him if he had ever heard Bob talking about bringing any sort of package from England to Norway.

Arne wrinkled his forehead and darted a compulsive look over his shoulder. No one there, of course.

'Lars mentioned this mysterious package on Tuesday night. No one knew anything about it.'

'What did Lars actually ask?'

'Just said you wanted to know if anyone had received a package from Bob Sherman.'

'And no one had?'

'No one who was there, anyway.'

'Could you write me a list of those who were there?'

'Yes,' he said with surprise. 'If you want it. But I can't see what it could possibly have to do with Bob's death.'

'I'm a great one for collecting useless information,' I said, smiling, and Arne gave me a look which said, oh yeah, plain as plain.

The races proceeded the same as before, except that the watching crowd was a good deal thinner than on Grand National day. The birch trees had dropped most of their yellow leaves and looked silver, the daylight was colder and greyer than ever, and a sharp wind whipped round every corner. But this time I had come prepared with a skiing cap with ear flaps and only my nose, like everyone else's, was turning blue.

Gunnar Holth saddled two for the hurdle race, hurrying busily from one to the other and juggling both sets of owners with anxious dexterity. One of his runners was the dappled mare with the uncertain temper, whose owner, Sven Wangen, was on Emma's list. Arne confirmed that the big young man assiduously hopping out of the way every time the mare presented her heels was indeed Sven Wangen, and added that the brunette sneering at him from a safe distance was his wife.

The jockey mounted warily and the mare bucked and kicked every inch to the start. Arne said that like all mean, bad-tempered females she would get her own way in the end, and went off to invest a little something on the Tote.

Wise move. She won. Arne beamed and said what did I tell you, when she comes here bitching she always wins. Was she ever docile? I asked, and Arne said sure, but those were her off days. We watched her being unsaddled in the winner's enclosure, with Gunnar Holth and Sven Wangen both tangoing smartly out of her way.

I told Arne I would like to meet Sven Wangen because Bob had ridden a winner for him on that last day. Arne showed reservations, so I asked him why.

He pursed his mouth. 'I don't like him. That's why.'

'What's wrong with him?'

'Too much money,' Arne said reprovingly. 'He behaves as if everyone ought to go on their knees when they talk to him. He has done nothing himself. The money was his father's. His father was a rich man. Too rich.'

'In what way too rich?'

Arne raised his eyebrows at what evidently seemed to him a nonsensical question, because from the tone of his reply it seemed he held great wealth to be morally wrong.

'He was a millionaire.'

'Don't you have millionaires in Norway?'

'Very few. They are not popular.'

I persuaded him, however, to introduce me to the unpopular Sven Wangen, whose father had made a million out of ships: and I saw at once why Arne didn't like him.

Perhaps two inches taller than I, he looked down his nose as if from a great height: and it was clear that this was no accidental mannerism but the manifestation of deep self-importance. Still probably in his twenties, he was bulky to the point of fatness and used his weight for throwing about. I didn't take to his manner, his small mouth, or his unfriendly light-amber eyes: nor, in fact, to his wife, who looked as if she could beat the difficult mare's temper by a couple of lengths.

Arne introduced me, and Sven Wangen saw no reason at all why I should call upon him at any time to ask him questions. He had heavy, rust-brown hair growing long over his ears, and a small flat cap which made his big head look bigger.

I said I understood he was a member of the racecourse committee which had asked me to come.

'Lars Baltzersen asked you,' he said brusquely. 'I was against it. I said so on Tuesday.'

'The sooner I get the questions answered, the sooner I'll go home,' I said. 'But not until.'

He looked at me with intense disfavour. 'What do you want, then?'

'Half an hour in your house,' I said. 'Any time that would suit you except for tomorrow afternoon.'

He settled in irritation for Sunday morning. His elegantly thin wife manufactured a yawn and they turned away without any pretence of politeness.

'See what I mean?' Arne said.

'I do indeed. Very unusual, wouldn't you say?'

'Unusual?'

'The rich don't usually behave like that.'

'Do you know so many rich people?' Arne asked with a touch of sarcasm.

'Meet them every day of the week,' I said. 'They own racehorses.'

Arne conceded that the rich weren't necessarily all beastly and went off on some official tasks. I tracked down Paddy O'Flaherty and found him with five minutes to spare between races.

'Brown envelope of blue pictures?' he repeated. 'He never said a dicky bird to me, now, about any blue pictures.' He grinned, and then an uncertain memory floated back. 'Wait now, I tell a lie. Back in the summer, now, he told me he had a good little tickle going for him, do you see? Always one for a chance at easy money, so he was. And there was this day, he winked at me like, and showed me the corner of an envelope in his overnight bag, and he said it would make our hair curl, so it would. So then I asked him for a look, do you see, but he said it was sealed some way so he couldn't steam it. I remember that, sure now I do.'

'The last time he came, did he say anything about bringing an envelope?'

Paddy shook his head. 'Like I said. Not a word.'

I thought. 'Did he come straight to your stable from the airport? Did he arrive on time, for instance?'

'I'll tell you something now. No, he didn't.' He concentrated. 'He was that late I thought he'd missed the flight and would come in the morning. Then, sure, a taxi rolls up and out he hops, large as life. He'd bought a bottle of brandy on the plane and there wasn't much left of that, now, before we went to bed.'

'What did he talk about?'

'Bejasus, how do I know, after all this time?'

'You must have thought often about that night.'

'Well, so I have, then.' He sighed at my perseverance, but thought some more. 'Horses, of course. We talked about horses. I don't remember him saying why he was late, or anything like that. And sure now I'd have thought it was the flight that was late, that was all.'

'I'll check,' I said:

'Look now, there was only one thing he said . . . Late on, when we'd maybe had a skinful, he said "Paddy, I think I've been conned." That's what he said now. "Paddy I think I've been conned." So I asked him what he meant, but he didn't tell me.'

'How insistently did you ask?'

'Insist . . .? Bejasus, of course I didn't. Uh . . . there

he was putting his finger over his mouth and nodding ... he was a bit tight, do you see? So I just put my finger over my mouth like him and I nodded just the same. Well now, it seemed sensible enough at the time do you see?'

I did see. It was a miracle Paddy remembered that evening at all.

The afternoon ambled on. Gunnar Holth won the steeplechase with Per Bjørn Sandvik's Whitefire, which displeased Rolf Torp, who was second. Per Bjørn, it appeared, had not come to the meeting: he rarely did on Thursdays, because it showed a bad example to his staff.

It was Lars Baltzersen who told me this, with warm approval in his voice. He himself, he said, had to leave his work only because he was Chairman, and all his employees understood. As one who had played lifelong truant at the drop of a starter's flag I found such noble standards a bit stifling, but one had to admire them.

Lars and I crossed the track and climbed the tower and looked down at the pond below. With its surface ruffled by the breeze it was far less peaceful than when I'd first seen it and just as brownly muddy as the day it gave up its dead. The swans and the ducks had gone.

'It will freeze soon,' Lars said. 'And snow will cover the racecourse for three or four months.'

'Bob Sherman is being buried today,' I said. 'In England.'

He nodded. 'We have sent a letter of regret to Mrs Sherman.'

'And a cheque,' I said; because his name too was on the list. He made a disclaiming movement with his hands but seemed genuinely pleased when I told him how much Emma had appreciated their kindness.

'I'm afraid we were all a little annoyed with her while she was here. She was so persistent. But perhaps it was partly because of her that we asked you to come. Anyway, I am glad she is not bitter about the way we tried to avoid her continual questions. She would have a right to be.'

'She isn't that sort of person.'

He turned his head to look at me. 'Do you know her well?' he asked.

'Only since all this started.'

'I regret the way we treated her,' he said. 'I think of it often. Giving her money does not buy us off.'

I agreed with him and offered no comfort. He looked away down the racecourse and I wondered if it was his guilty conscience that had driven him to persuade me back.

After the next race, a long distance flat race, we walked across together to the weighing room.

I said, 'You were in the officials' room that day when Bob Sherman poked his head in and could have seen the money lying on the floor.'

'That's right,' Lars said.

'Well . . . what was the question?'

He was puzzled. 'What question?'

'Everyone's statement to the police was the same. You all said "Bob Sherman came to the door asking some question or other." So . . . what was the question?'

He looked deeply surprised. 'It can't have had anything to do with his disappearance.'

'What was it?'

'I can't remember. Nothing of the slightest importance, I assure you, or of course we would have told the police.'

We rejoined Arne, and Lars asked him if he by any chance remembered what Bob had wanted. Arne looked just as surprised and said he had no idea, he'd been busy anyway and probably hadn't even heard. The racecourse manager however knew that he had known once, because it was he who had answered.

'Let me think,' he said, frowning. 'He came in . . . not his feet, just his head and shoulders. He looked down at the money, which was lying in front of him. I remember that distinctly. I told the police. But the question . . . it was nothing.'

I shrugged. 'Tell me if you ever remember?'

He said he would as if he thought it unlikely, but an hour later he sought me out.

'Bob Sherman asked if Mikkel Sandvik had already gone home, and I said I didn't know.'

'Oh.'

He laughed. 'Well, we did tell you it was nothing important.'

'And you were right.' I sighed resignedly. 'It was just a chance.'

At the end of the afternoon Lars took me up to his Chairman's room to give me the copies the police had provided of their Bob Sherman file. He stood in front of the big stove, a neat, substantial figure in his heavy, dark blue overcoat and ear-flapped astrakhan hat, blowing on his fingers.

'Cold today,' he said.

I thought I probably knew him better than anyone I'd met in Norway, but all the same I said, 'May I call to see you in your office?'

He'd heard about my appointments and smiled wryly at being included. 'Saturday, if you like. I'll be there until noon.'

Declining a pressing invitation from Arne to dine with him and Kari, I ate early at the Grand and went upstairs to do my homework.

The police had been painstaking, but the net result, as Lars had said, was nil.

A long and immensely detailed autopsy report, filled with medical terms I only half understood, concluded that the deceased had died of three overlapping depressed fractures of the skull. Unconsciousness would have been immediate. Death followed a few minutes later: the exact interval could not be specified. Immersion was subsequent to death.

The nylon rope found on the deceased had been unravelled strand by strand, and an analysis had indicated it to be part of a batch manufactured the previous spring and distributed during the summer to countless shops and ships' chandlers throughout greater Oslo.

The nylon rope found embedded in a concrete block in the Øvrevoll pond was of identical composition.

The cement block itself was a sort of sandbag in widespread use for sea-walling. The type in the pond was very common, and none of the contractors currently using it could remember having one stolen. The writer of the report added his own personal opinion that no contractor would ever miss one single bag out of hundreds.

The properties of the bag were such that its ingredients were crumbly when dry, but solidified like rock under water. The nylon rope had been tied tightly round the cement bag while it had still been dry.

Extensive inquiries had dug up no one who had heard or seen any activity round the pond on either the night of the deceased's disappearance or the night he had been removed from the water. The night watchman had proved a dead loss. There were lists of everything they had found in Bob Sherman's pockets and in his overnight bag. Clothes, watch, keys were all as they should be: it was papers I was interested in, and they, after a month submerged, were in a pretty pulpy state.

Passport and air ticket had been identified. Currency notes had been nearly all British: total value fifteen pounds sterling. There had been no Norwegian money to speak of, and certainly not five canvas bags of it.

The report made no mention of any papers or ruins of papers being found in the overnight bag. Nor of photographs: and photographic paper fared better than most under water.

I read everything through twice and drew no conclusions which the police hadn't. Bob Sherman had had his head bashed in, and later he'd been roped to a cement bag and dumped in the pond. By person or persons unknown.

By person or persons who were doing their damndest, also, to remain unknown.

I lifted the polythene-wrapped knife from my sponge case and propped it against the reading lamp; and immediately the slice down my chest took up throbbing where it had left off that morning. Why was it, I wondered irritably, that cuts only throbbed at night?

It was as well though to have that to remind me not to walk trustingly into hotel rooms or hail the first taxi that offered. Business had been meant in London, and I saw no safety in Oslo.

I smiled ruefully to myself. I was getting as bad as Arne at looking over my shoulder.

But there could be a lot more knives where that one came from.

CHAPTER TEN

In the morning I took the knife along to the police and told them how I'd come by it. The man in charge of the case, the same policeman who had been overseeing the dragging of the pond, looked at me in a sort of startled dismay.

'We will try to trace it, as you ask. But this knife is not rare. There are many knives of this kind. In English those words *Norsk Stål* on the blade merely mean Norwegian steel.'

His name was Lund. His air that of long-term policemen everywhere: cautious, watchful, friendly with reservations. It seemed to me that many policemen were only completely at ease with criminals; and certainly the ex-policemen who worked for the investigation branch of the Jockey Club always spoke of petty crooks more affectionately than of the general public.

Dedicated to catching them, policemen also admired criminals. They spoke the same language, used the same jargon. I knew from observation that if a crook and a detective who didn't know each other turned up at the same social gathering, they would unerringly seek each other out. Unless one of them happened to be chasing the other at that moment, they would get on well together; a fact which explained the apparently extraordinary shared holidays which occasionally scandalized the press.

Lund treated me with scrupulous fairness as a temporary colleague. I thanked him warmly for letting me use his files, and he offered help if I should need it.

I said at once that I needed a car with a driver I could trust, and could he recommend one.

He looked at the knife lying on his desk.

'I cannot lend you a police car.' He thought it over, then picked up a telephone, gave some Norwegian instructions, put down the receiver, and waited.

'I will ask my brother to drive you,' he said. 'He is an author. His books make little money. He will be pleased to earn some for driving, because he likes driving.'

The telephone buzzed and Lund evidently put forward his proposition. I gathered that it met with the author's approval because Lund asked when I would like him to start.

'Now,' I said. 'I'd like him to collect me here.'

Lund nodded, put down the receiver, and said, 'He will be here in half an hour. You will find him helpful. He speaks English very well. He worked once in England.'

I spent the half hour looking through mug-shots, but my London assailant was nowhere to be seen.

Lund's brother Erik was a bonus in every way.

He met me in the front hall with a vague distracted grin as if he had been waiting for someone else. A tallish man of about fifty-five, he had sparse, untidy blond hair, a shapeless old sports jacket, and an air of being totally disorganized: and he drove, I soon discovered, as if other cars were invisible.

He waved me from the police building to a small-sized cream Volvo waiting at the kerb. Dents and scratches of varying rust vintages bore witness to long and sturdy service, and the boot was held shut by string. Upon opening the passenger-side door I found that most of the interior was already occupied by a very large Great Dane.

'Lie down, Odin,' Erik said hopefully, but the huge dog understood no English, remained on his feet, and slobbered gently down my neck.

'Where first?' Erik asked. His English, as his brother had said, was splendid. He settled himself in the driver's seat and looked at me expectantly.

'What did your brother tell you?' I asked.

'To drive you around and if possible make sure no one bumps you off.' He said it as casually as if he'd been entrusted to see me on to the right train.

'What are you good at?' I said curiously.

'Driving, boxing and telling tales out of school.'

He had a long face, deeply lined round the eyes, smoother round mouth and chin: evidence of a nature more at home with a laugh than a scowl. In the course of the next few days I learnt that if it hadn't been for his highly developed sense of the ludicrous, he would have been a dedicated communist. As it was he held good radical left wing views, but found himself in constant despair over the humourlessness of his fellow travellers. He had worked on the gossip pages of newspapers throughout his youth, and had spent two years in Fleet Street; and he told me more about the people he was driving me to visit than I would have dug out in six weeks.

'Per Bjørn Sandvik?' he repeated, when I told him our first destination. 'The upright man of the oil fields?'

'I guess so,' I said.

He took off into the traffic without waiting for a gap. I opened my mouth and shut it again: after all, if his brother was trusting him to keep me alive, the least I could do was let him get on with it. We swung round some hair-raising corners on two wheels but pulled up unscathed outside the main offices of Norsk Oil Imports Ltd. The Great Dane licked his great chops and looked totally unmoved.

'There you are,' Erik said, pointing to an imposing double-door entrance into a courtyard. 'Through there, turn left, big entrance with pillars.'

'You know it?'

He nodded. 'I know most places in Oslo. And most people.' And he told me about his years on the newspapers.

'Tell me about Per Bjørn, then.'

He smiled. 'He is stuffy, righteous, and has given himself to big business. During the war he wasn't like that at all. When we were all young, he was a great fighter against the Nazis, a great planner and saboteur. But the years go by and he has solidified into a dull lump, like the living core of a volcano pouring out and dying to dry, grey pumice.'

'He must have some fire left,' I objected. 'To be the head of an oil company.'

He blew down his nostrils in amusement. 'All the oil companies in Norway are tied hand and foot by government regulations, which is as it should be. There is no room for private speculation. Per Bjørn can only make decisions within a small area. For anything above ordering new ashtrays he has to have permission from the government.'

'You approve of that?'

'Naturally.'

'What do you know about his family?' I asked.

His eyes glimmered. 'He married a thoroughly boring plain girl called Ragnhild whose dad just happened at that time to be the head man in Norsk Oil Imports.'

I grinned and climbed out of the car, and told him I would be half an hour at least.

'I brought a book,' he said equably, and pulled a tattered paperback of *The Golden Notebook* out of his jacket pocket.

The courtyard, tidily paved, had a stone-edged bed of frostbitten flowers in the centre and distinguished pale yellow buildings all round the edge. The main entrance to the left was imposing, and opposite, to the right, stood a similar entrance on a much smaller scale. The wall facing the entrance from the street was pierced with tall windows and decorated with shutters, and the whole opulent little square looked more like a stately home than an oil company's office.

It was, I found, both.

Per Bjørn's secretary fielded me from the main entrance, shovelled me up one flight of carpeted stairs and into his office, told me Mr Sandvik was still at a meeting but would not be long, and went away.

Although the building was old the head man's room was modern, functional, and highly Scandinavian, with thickly double-glazed windows looking down into the courtyard. On the wall hung a simple chart of a rock formation with layers labelled impermeable, source, permeable and reservoir; a list saying things like spudded Oct 71, plugged and abandoned Jan 72; and three brightly coloured maps of the North Sea, each of them showing a different aspect of the oil drilling operations going on there.

In each map the sea area was subdivided along lines of latitude and longitude into small squares which were labelled 'Shell', 'Esso', 'Conoco', and so on, but although I looked carefully I could see none marked Norsk Oil Imports.

The door opened behind me and Per Bjørn Sandvik came in, as pleasant and easy as ever and giving every impression of having got to the top without pushing.

'David,' he said in his high clear diction, 'sorry to keep you waiting.'

'Just looking at your maps,' I said.

He nodded, crossing to join me. 'We're drilling there . . . and there.' He pointed to two areas which bore an entirely different name. I commented on it, and he explained.

'We are part of a consortium. There are no private oil companies in Norway.'

'What did Norsk Oil Imports do before anyone discovered oil under the North Sea?'

'Imported oil, of course.'

'Of course.'

I smiled and sat down in the square armchair he indicated.

'Fire away,' he said, 'with the questions.'

'Did Bob Sherman bring you any papers or photographs from England?'

He shook his head. 'No. Lars asked us this on Tuesday. Sherman did not bring any papers for anyone.' He stretched out a hand towards his desk intercom. 'Would you like some coffee?'

'Very much.'

He nodded and asked his secretary to arrange it.

'All the same,' I said, 'he probably did bring a package of some sort with him, and he probably did pass it on. If anyone would admit to having received it we might be able to take it out of consideration altogether.'

He stared vaguely at his desk.

'For instance,' I said, 'if what he brought was straight pornography, it probably had nothing to do with his death.'

He looked up.

'I see,' he said. 'And because no one has said they received it, you think it did not contain pornography?'

'I don't know what it contained,' I said. 'I wish I did.'

The coffee arrived and he poured it carefully into dark brown crusty mugs.

'Have you discarded the idea that Bob Sherman was killed by whoever stole the money?'

'It's in abeyance,' I said, refusing the offered cream and sugar. 'Could you give me your impression of Bob Sherman as a man?'

He bunched his lips assessingly.

'Not over-intelligent,' he said. 'Honest, but easily influenced. A good rider, of course. He always rode well for me.'

'I gather Rolf Torp thought he rode a bad race for him that last day.'

Sandvik delicately shrugged. 'Rolf is sometimes hard to please.'

We drank the coffee and talked about Bob, and after a while I said I would like very much to meet Per Bjørn's son, Mikkel.

He frowned. 'To ask him questions?'

'Well . . . some. He knew Bob comparatively well, and he's the one good contact I've not yet met.'

He didn't like it. 'I can't stop you, of course. Or at least, I won't. But he has been very upset by the whole affair, first by thinking his friend was a thief, and now more since he knows he was murdered.'

'I'll try not to worry him too much. I've read his short statement to the police. I don't expect to do much more than cover the same ground.'

'Then why bother him at all?'

After a pause to consider it, I said, 'I think I need to see him, to get the picture of Bob's visits complete.'

He slowly sucked his lower lip but finally made no more objections.

'He's at boarding school now,' he said. 'But he'll be home here for the afternoon tomorrow. If you come at three, he'll be here.'

'Here . . . in your office?'

He shook his head. 'In my house. The other side of the courtyard.'

I stood up to go and thanked him for his time.

'I haven't been of much use,' he said. 'We've given you a pretty hopeless job.'

'Oh well . . .' I said, and told myself that things some-times broke if one hammered on long enough. 'I'll do my best to earn your money.'

He saw me to the top of the stairs and shook hands.

'Let me know if there's anything I can do.'

'I will,' I said. 'And thank you.'

I walked down the quiet stairs to the large empty hall. The only sounds of life seemed to come from behind a door at the back of the hall, so I walked over and opened it.

It led, I found, straight into the next door building, one dedicated not to front offices but to getting the paper work done. Even there, however, things were going at a gentle pace without any feeling of pressure, and in the doorways of the row of small offices stretch-ing away from me stood relaxed people in sweaters drinking coffee and smoking and generally giving no impression that commercial life was rushing by.

I retreated through the hall, through the courtyard, and back to Erik Lund. He withdrew his eyes from his Golden Notes as I climbed into his car and appeared to be wondering who I was.

Recognition of sorts awoke.

'Oh yes . . .' he said.

'Lunch, then?' I suggested.

He had few definite views on where to eat, but once we were installed in a decent restaurant he lost no time in ordering something he called *gravlaks*. The price made me wince on behalf of the racecourse, but I had

153

some too, and it proved to be the most exquisite form of salmon, cured instead of smoked.

'Are you from Scotland Yard?' he asked after the last of the pink heaven had been dispatched.

'No. From the Jockey Club.'

It surprised him, so I explained briefly why I was there.

'What's all this about being bumped off, then?'

'To stop me finding out what happened.'

He gazed past me in thought.

'Makes my brother Knut a dumb cluck, doesn't it? No one's tried to get rid of *him*.'

'Knock down one policeman and six more pop up,' I said.

'And there aren't six more of you?' he asked dryly.

'The racing cupboard's pretty bare.'

He drank coffee thoughtfully. 'Why don't you give it up while you're still whole?'

'Natural bloody obstinacy,' I said. 'What do you know about Rolf Torp?'

'Rolf Torp the terror of the ski slopes or Rolf Torp who designs glass houses for pygmies?'

'Rolf Torp who owns racehorses and does something in mines.'

'Oh. Him.' He frowned, sniffed, and grimaced. 'Another goddam capitalist exploiting the country's natural resources for private gain.'

'Do you know anything about him personally?'

'Isn't that personal enough?'

'No.'

He laughed. 'You don't think money-grubbing says anything about a man's soul?'

'Everything any man does says something about his soul.'

'You wriggle out of things,' he said.

'And things out of people.'

'Well,' he said smiling, 'I can't actually tell you much about that Rolf Torp. For one thing I've never met him, and for another, capitalists make dull copy for gossip columns unless they're caught in bed with their secretaries and no pyjamas.'

Blue pictures for blackmail, I thought irrelevantly. Or black and white pictures for blackmail. Why not?

'Do you know anyone called Lars Baltzersen?' I asked.

'Sure. The Chairman of Øvrevoll? Every man's idea of a respectable pillar of society. Entertains ambassadors and presents prizes. Often a picture on the sports pages, always beside the man of the moment. Mind you, our Lars was a live wire once himself. Did a lot of motor racing, mostly in Sweden. That was before banking finally smothered him, of course.'

'Family?'

'Dutch wife, lots of solid children.'

I paid the bill and we strolled back to the car. Odin stared out of the front window with his huge head close to the glass and his eyes unblinking. Some people who stopped to try 'isn't-he-a-nice-boy' noises got a big yawn and a view down a cavernous throat.

Erik opened his door, gave the dog a shove and said, '*Fanden ta dig.*' The Dane shifted his bulk towards the back seat without taking offence, and the journey continued.

'What did Lars do in the war?'

'He wasn't here,' he said promptly. 'He was in London, reading the news in Norwegian on the radio.'

'He didn't tell me he'd lived in London.'

'He's quiet now. Another dead volcano. More pumice.'

Erik crossed some traffic lights three seconds after they turned red and genuinely didn't seem to hear six other motorists grinding their brake drums to screaming point. Odin gave him an affectionate nudge in the neck and Erik put out the hand he needed on the gear lever and fondled the huge wet nose.

He pulled up in front of a modern square-built glass and slab affair a mile out of the city centre, a far cry from Sandvik's architectural elegance.

'This is the address you gave me,' Erik said dubiously.

'Fine,' I said. 'Would you like to wait inside?'

He shook his head, though the afternoon was cold and rapidly growing dark. 'Odin gives off heat like a nuclear reactor and I don't like sitting in plastic lobbies being stared at.'

'OK.'

I left them to their companionship and rode a lift up to Rolf Torp's office, where again as I was early I was asked to wait. This time not in Torp's own office, but a small purpose-decorated room overflowing with useful handouts about 'Torp-Nord Associates'.

The walls here also were hung with diagrams of rock formations, charts of progress and maps showing areas being worked. These maps were not of the North Sea but of the mainland, with the thickest cluster of work-tags to the west of Oslo, in the mountains.

Someone had told me Rolf Torp's business was silver, but it wasn't or no longer chiefly. His associates had switched to titanium.

Before he finally turned up (at four twenty) for his four o'clock appointment I had learnt a good deal I didn't especially want to know about titanium. For example that it weighed only 0.163 lb per cubic inch and in alloy form could reach a tensile strength of 200,000 lb per square inch. Bully for titanium, I thought.

Rolf Torp was much like his product in tensile strength but couldn't match it for lightness. He made no effort to conceal that my visit was a nuisance, bursting into the waiting room saying, 'Come on, come on then. I can give you ten minutes, that's all,' and stomping off to his own office without waiting to see if I followed.

I did, of course. His office was much like Sandvik's: same type of furniture, fabrics and carpet, a reflection of prevailing style but no clue to the occupant. The walls here were dotted with framed photographs of various stages of metal production, and another large map with thumb tacks took pride of place.

'How do you mine titanium?' I asked, and sat in the visitors' chair without being invited. Irritably he took his own place behind half an acre of tidy desk and lit a cigarette.

'Like one?' he said belatedly, pushing a box towards me.

'No, thank you.'

He flicked a lighter and deeply inhaled the smoke.

'You don't find titanium lying around like coal,' he said. 'Are you sure you want to use your ten minutes on this?'

'Might as well.'

He gave me a puzzled look over the heavy black moustache, but seemed to find his own subject a lot less temper-disturbing than mine.

'Titanium is the ninth most common element on earth. It is found in ninety-eight per cent of rocks and also in oil, coal, water, plants, animals, and stars.'

'You can hardly dig it out of people.'

'No. It is mostly mined as a mineral called ilmenite . . . which is one third titanium.'

'Does your firm do the actual mining?'

He shook his head. 'We survey, do first drillings, advise and establish.'

I looked vaguely at the photographs on the walls.

'Apart from high speed aircraft, what's the stuff used for?'

He reeled off technical uses as if he'd been asked that one once or twice before. Towards the end, slowing down, he included paint, lipstick and smokescreens. There was little you couldn't do, it seemed, with the strength of the Titans.

'Did Bob Sherman bring you any photographs?'

I asked him casually without looking at him directly, but if it jerked him at all I couldn't tell, as he swept any involuntary movement into a quick gesture to flick off ash.

'No, he didn't.'

'Did he ask your advice about anything?'

'Why should he?'

'People do need advice sometimes,' I said.

He gave a laugh that was half a scowl. 'I gave him some. He didn't ask. I told him to ride races better or stay in England.'

'He didn't please you?'

'He should have won on my good horse. He went to sleep. He stopped trying to win, and he was beaten. Also he did not ride as I told him, all the way round.'

'Do you think someone bribed him to lose?'

He looked startled. For all his bad-tempered criticism it hadn't occurred to him, and to be fair, he didn't pounce on the idea.

'No,' he said heavily. 'He wanted to ride that horse in the Grand National. It started favourite and it won.'

I nodded. 'I saw the race.'

'That's right. Bob Sherman wanted to ride it, but I would have got someone else anyway. He rode it very badly.'

I imagined that any time Rolf Torp's jockey didn't win, he had automatically ridden badly. I stood up to go, which puzzled him again, and shook his hand.

'Coming here has been a waste of your time,' he said.

'Of course not . . . I'll let myself out.'

He didn't stop me. I closed his door and did a brief exploration. More offices. More bustle than at Sandvik's. More impression of work being done, but nothing so earthy as a lump of ore.

Erik was not parked out front where I had left him. I went through the big glass entrance doors, peered briefly into the darkness, and ignominiously retreated. One thing I did not plan to do was walk around at night alone, making everything easy for assassins.

After ten minutes I began to wonder if he'd simply forgotten about me and gone home, but he hadn't. The small cream Volvo returned at high speed and stopped outside in its own length. Its owner extricated himself from the quivering metal and strolled towards the building.

'Hullo,' he said, as I met him. 'Hope you haven't

been waiting. I had to get Odin's dinner. Forgot all about it.'

In the car, Odin loomed hungrily over my head, dribbling. Just as well, I thought, that he was about to be fed.

Erik returned us to the Grand at tar-melting speed and seemed disappointed that I hadn't wanted any longer journeys.

CHAPTER ELEVEN

The receptionists of the Grand considered me totally mad because I was insisting on changing my room every day, but they would have thought me even madder if I'd told them the reason. I asked them just to allocate me the last empty room, or if there were several, to give me a random choice at bed time. They did it with politely glazed eyes while I thankfully put my trust in unpredictability.

When Erik dropped me at the door and took his big friend home I telephoned to Arne and Kari and asked them to dinner.

'Come here,' Kari demanded warmly, but I said it was time I repaid their kindness, and after much demur they agreed to the Grand. I sat in the bar and read a newspaper until they arrived, and thought about growing old.

It was strange, but away from her chosen setting, Kari looked a different person. Not so young, not so domesticated, not so tranquil. This Kari, walking with assurance into the bar in a long black skirt and white ruffled shirt was the woman who designed interiors as a business. This Kari, wearing perfect make-up, diamonds in her ears and hair smoothly pinned up, looked at once cooler and more mature than the casual home-girl. When she put a smooth sweet-smelling cheek forward for a kiss and gave me a pretty look from under her lashes I found I both liked her less and wanted her more; both of which reactions were disconcerting and no good.

Arne was Arne, the antithesis of a chameleon, his personality so concretely formed that it retained its own shape whatever the environment. He swept four-square into the bar and gave it a quick suspicious survey to make sure no one could listen at his shoulder.

'Hallo David,' he said, shaking my hand vigorously. 'What have you been doing all day?'

'Wasting time,' I said smiling, 'and wondering what to do next.'

We sat in a comfortable corner and drank (as for once it was the right hour on the right day) whisky.

Arne wanted to know what progress I had made.

'Not much,' I said. 'You might practically say none.'

'It must be very difficult,' Kari said sympathetically, with Arne nodding in agreement. 'How do you know what to look for?'

'I don't often look for things. I look at what's there.'

'All detectives look for things. Look for clues and follow trails. Of course they do.'

'And trudge up dead ends and find red herrings,' I said.

'Herrings are not red,' Kari said in puzzlement.

Fifty-seven varieties of herring in Norway, and not one of them red.

'A red herring is something that doesn't exist,' Arne said, but had to explain it again to her in Norwegian.

She laughed, but returned to her questions. 'How do you solve a crime?'

'Um . . . you think what you might have done if you'd been the crook, and then you look to see if that's what he did. And sometimes it is.'

'No one else solves crimes like David,' Arne said.

'Believe me,' I said. 'They do.'

'What do you think the crook did this time?' Kari asked.

I looked at her clear grey eyes, asking the question I couldn't answer without freezing the evening in its tracks.

'There's more than one,' I said neutrally. 'Emma Sherman saw two.'

We talked about Emma for a while. Arne had met her grandfather during his brief visit, and knew he had not been able to identify either of the intruders.

'And nobody knows what they were looking for,' Kari said thoughtfully.

'The men knew,' I said.

Arne's eyes stretched suddenly wide, which made a change from blinking. 'So they did,' he said.

'Of course they did,' she said. 'I don't see the point.'

'It isn't really a point. Only that someone somewhere does know what is missing. Or what was missing, because it may have been found now.'

Kari thought it over. 'Why do you think they didn't search the Shermans' house at once, as soon as they'd killed Bob Sherman? Why wait a month?'

Arne went back to blinking fit to bust, but he left it to me to answer.

'I think,' I said, 'it was because Bob Sherman was found, and whatever it was that was missing wasn't found with him.' I paused. 'Say Mr X kills Bob and dumps him in the pond, for a reason as yet unknown. Suppose this was after Bob delivered a package he had been bringing with him. Suppose also that Bob had opened the package and taken out some of the contents, but that Mr X did not discover this until after he'd killed Bob and put him in the pond. OK so far? So then he has to guess whether Bob had the missing contents in his pockets or his overnight bag, in which case they too are safely in the pond, or whether he passed them on to someone else, or even posted them home to himself in England, before he was killed. Short of getting Bob out of the pond, Mr X can't find out for certain, but the longer the missing contents don't turn up, the surer Mr X becomes that they are with Bob. Right. But then Bob is found, and the missing contents are still missing. So a search party is sent out to find out if Bob took them out of the package at home before he even left England, and Emma was unfortunate enough to choose just that moment to go back for some fresh clothes.'

Kari's mouth had slowly opened. 'Wow,' she said. 'And it seemed such a simple little question.'

'I told you,' Arne said. 'Give him one fact and he guesses the rest.'

'And a guess is all it is.' I smiled. 'I don't know why they took a month to start searching. Do you?'

Kari said 'But you must be right. It sounds so reasonable.'

'Like the earth is flat.'

'What?'

'Sounds reasonable until you know different.'

We went in to dinner. There was an orchestra playing, and dancing, and later, with the coffee, a singer. It was all too much in the end for Arne who stood up abruptly, said he needed some air, and made a compulsive dash for the door.

We watched his retreating back.

'Has he always been like that?' I asked.

'Always since I've known him. Though lately, perhaps, it has been worse. He used not to worry about bugging machines.'

'He used not to know they existed.'

'Well . . . that's true.'

'How did it start? His persecution complex, I mean.'

'Oh . . . the war, I suppose. When he was a child. I wasn't born until after, but Arne was a child then. His grandfather was shot as a hostage, and his father was in the resistance. Arne says he was always frightened when he was a child, but he wasn't always sure what he was frightened of. Sometimes his father sent him to run with messages and told him to be sure not to be followed. Arne says he was always terrified those times that he would turn round and find a big man behind him.'

'Poor Arne,' I said.

'He has been to psychiatrists,' Kari said. 'He knows . . . but he still can't help it.' She looked away from me, at the couples slowly circling on the square of polished floor. 'He can't bear dancing.'

After a few seconds I said, 'Would you like to?'

'I don't suppose he'd mind.'

She stood up without hesitation and danced with natural rhythm. She also knew quite well that I liked having her close: I could see it in her eyes. I wondered if she'd ever been unfaithful to Arne, or ever would be. I wondered about the age-old things. One can't help it, I find.

She smiled and moved forward until our bodies were touching at more points than not, and no woman ever did that unless she meant to. What we were engaged in from that moment on was an act of sex: upright, dancing, public and fully clothed, but an act of sex none the less. I knew theoretically that a woman could reach a vivid orgasm without actual intercourse, that in fact some could do it when all alone simply by thinking erotic thoughts, but I had never before seen it happen.

It happened to Kari because she wanted it to. Because she rubbed closely against me with every turn of the dance. Because I didn't expect it. Because I didn't push her off.

Her breathing grew slower and deeper and her eyes lost their brightness. Her mouth was closed, half smiling. Head up, neck straight, she looked more withdrawn and absent-minded than passionately aroused. Then quite suddenly her whole body flushed with heat, and behind her eyes and right through her very deep I was for almost twenty seconds aware of a gentle intense throbbing.

After that she took a great deep gulping breath as if her lungs had been cramped. Her mouth opened, the smile broadened, and she unplastered herself from my front.

Her eyes grew bright as stars, and she laughed into mine.

'Thank you,' she said.

She had finished with dancing. She broke away and walked back to the table, sitting down sociably as if nothing had happened. Oh thanks very much, I thought, and where does that leave me? Dealing with an unscratchable itch and without the later comfort of doing it on my own like she had, because I'd never found that much fun.

'More coffee?' I said. One had to say something, I

supposed. How about 'Damn your eyes you selfish little pig'?

'Thank you,' she said.

The waiter brought more coffee. Civilization won the day.

Arne returned looking windblown and a little happier. Kari put her hand on his with wifely warmth and understanding, and I remembered ironically that I had wondered if she were ever unfaithful to him. She was and she wasn't: the perfect recipe for having it both ways.

They left shortly afterwards, pressing me to spend another evening at their flat before I went home.

'See you on Sunday at Øvrevoll,' Arne said. 'If not before.'

When they had gone I collected my suitcase from the hall porter and took myself to the reception desk. There were five empty rooms to choose from, so I took a key at random and got myself a spacious double room with a balcony looking out towards the parliament building. I opened the well-closed double doors and let a blast from the Arctic play havoc with the central heating. Then I shut them again and went coldly to bed, and lay awake for a long time thinking about a lot of things but hardly at all about Kari.

Erik came to breakfast the next morning. He joined me with a grin, helped himself to half a ton of assorted pickled fish from the buffet, and ate as if there were no tomorrow.

'Where to?' he asked after two further bread rolls, four slices of cheese and several cups of coffee.

'Øvrevoll,' I said.

'But there's no racing today.'

'I know.'

'Well, if that's what you want, let's go.'

Odin, in a friendly mood, sat centrally with his rump wedged against the rear seat and his front paws and huge head burying the handbrake. When Erik gave him a nudge with his elbow the dog lifted his chin long enough for his master to release the wheels. A double act of long standing, it seemed.

The journey was a matter of staring death in the face, but we got there. The main gates of the racecourse stood open with various trade vans standing inside on the tarmac, so we simply drove in and stopped near the weighing room. Erik and Odin unfolded themselves and stretched their legs while I went on my short and abortive mission.

There were cleaners, a man and two women, in the weighing room building, and none of them spoke English. I went outside and cajoled Erik, the easiest task on earth, to do my talking.

He asked, listened, and passed on the bad news.

'They say Bob Sherman's saddle was here for a long time. In the changing room, on the peg nearest the corner.'

I had just looked all round the changing room. No saddles on any pegs and no trace of Bob Sherman's.

'They say it went at about the time the body was found in the pond. They don't know who took it.'

'That's that, then.'

We left the weighing room building and strolled the few yards to the racecourse rails. The morning was icy, the wind fresh, the trees sighing. Winter on the doorstep, snow on the way.

Down the sand track Gunnar Holth's string was starting a canter, and as we watched they came up fast towards us and swept past along to the winning post and round the top of the course where the pond lay. Paddy O'Flaherty in his brilliant woollen cap rode in front, giving a lead and setting the pace. With racing the next day, it was little more than a pipe-opener, and the string presently slowed to walk home.

'Next stop,' I said, 'is Gunnar Holth's stable.'

We drew up in the yard as the horses came back from the track, steaming like kettles under their rugs. Gunnar Holth himself jumped down from Sandvik's Whitefire, patted him vigorously, and waited for me to open the game.

'Morning,' I said.

'Morning.'

'Can we talk?'

He nodded resignedly, led Whitefire off into the barn, returned, jerked his head towards his bungalow and opened his door. Erik this time chose to stay in the car for which Gunnar Holth, having spotted Odin, looked thankful.

'Coffee?'

Same orange pot on the stove. Same coffee, I dared say.

'I am looking for Bob Sherman's saddle,' I said.

'His saddle? Didn't he leave it behind? I heard he did . . .'

'I wondered if you knew who had it. I want to find it . . . It belongs to his wife now.'

'And saddles are worth money,' he said, nodding. 'I haven't seen it. I don't know who has it.'

I asked him obliquely twice more in different ways but in the end was satisfied that he knew nothing helpful.

'I'll ask Paddy,' I said. But Paddy too had few ideas.

'It was there, so it was, until they pulled the poor devil out of the water. Sure I saw it there myself on Grand National day. Then the next meeting, on the Thursday, it was gone.'

'Are you sure of that?'

'As sure as I'm standing here.'

I said mildly, 'Why? Why are you so sure?'

His eyes flickered. 'Well . . . as to that, now . . .'

'Paddy,' I said. 'Come clean.'

'Uh . . .'

'Did you take it?'

'No,' he said positively. 'That I did not.' The idea apparently outraged him.

'What, then?'

'Well now then, do you see, he was after being a real mate of mine, Bob was . . . Well I was sure now, in my own mind, that he would want me to do it . . .' He ran down and stopped.

'To do what?'

'Look now, it wasn't stealing or anything like that.'

'Paddy, what did you do?'

'Well . . . there was my helmet, see, and there was his helmet, hanging there with his saddle. Well now, my helmet had a strap broken, so it had, and Bob's was there, good as new, so I just swapped them over, do you see . . .'

'And that was on Grand National day?'

'That's right. And the next race day, after Bob was found, his saddle was gone. And my helmet was gone with it, do you see.'

'So Bob's helmet is . . . here?'

'It is so. In my box, now, under my bunk.'

'Will you lend it to me for a while?'

'Lend it?' He was surprised. 'I thought you'd be taking it away altogether, now, as by rights it belongs to his missus.'

'I expect she'd be glad for you to keep it.'

'It's a good helmet, so it is.'

He went and fetched it and handed it over, an ordinary regulation jockey helmet with a chin strap. I thanked him, told him I'd let him have it back, waved goodbye to Gunnar Holth, and set off on the perilous passage back to central Oslo.

In between bounces I pulled out the padded lining of the helmet and looked underneath. No photographs, papers or other missing objects. Nothing but black regulation padding. I put it back into place.

'No good?' Erik said sympathetically, peering round Odin.

'All stones have to be turned.'

'Which stone next, then?'

'Lars Baltzersen.'

The route to his bank lay past the front door of the Grand, so I stopped off there and left Bob Sherman's helmet with the hall porter, who was already sheltering my newly re-packed suitcase. He told me he would take good care of anything I left with him. I left three ten-kroner notes with him, and with a smile he took good care of those.

Lars had almost given up.

'Thought you'd changed your mind,' he said, showing me into his office.

'Had to make a detour,' I said, apologizing.

'Well, now that you are here . . .' He produced a bottle of red wine and two small glasses from a discreet cupboard, and poured for us both.

His room, like Sandvik's and Torp's, was standard Scandinavian, modern vintage. Commerce, I supposed, must be seen to be up to date, but as a source of personal information these interiors were a dead loss.

No maps on his walls. Pictures of houses, factories, office blocks, distant ports. When I asked him, he told me that his banking firm was chiefly concerned with the financing of industrial projects.

'Merchant banking,' he said. 'Also we run a building scheme very like an English building society. Except that here, of course, we lend at a much lower interest rate, so that mortgages are cheaper.'

'Don't the investors complain?'

'They get almost the same return as British investors. It is just that Norwegian societies don't have to pay big taxes. It is the tax which puts up the British mortgage rate.'

He told me that there were many small private banks in Norway running building schemes, but that his own was one of the largest.

'There is a terrible shortage of building land round Oslo,' he said. 'Young couples find it very difficult to find a house. Yet far out in the country there are whole farms standing empty and derelict. The old people have died or are too weak to work the fields, and the young people have left the hard life and gone to the towns.'

'Same everywhere,' I said.

He liked wooden houses best, he said. 'They breathe.'

'How about fire?' I asked.

'It always used to be a fearful risk. Cities were burnt sometimes. But now our fire services are so fast, so expert, that I am told if you want to burn your house for the insurance, you have to hose it down with petrol. Otherwise the fire will be put out at the first puff of smoke.'

We drank the wine and Lars smoked a cigarette. I asked him about his years in London and about his motor racing in Sweden, but he seemed to have no interest left in them.

'The past is over,' he said. 'It is banking and Øvrevoll which I think about now.'

He asked me if I yet knew who killed Bob Sherman. Such faith in the way he put it.

'Not yet,' I said. 'What's my limit on expenses?'

I couldn't pin him to an amount. It seemed that if I succeeded there was no limit. If I failed, I had already overspent.

'Have you any ideas?' he asked.

'Ideas aren't enough.'

'You need proof as well, I suppose.'

'Mm . . . have to make like a poacher.'

'What do you mean?'

'Set traps,' I said. 'And keep my feet out of other poachers' snares.'

I stood up to go. He too said my visit had been a waste of time because he had told me nothing useful.

'You never know,' I said.

Erik and I had lunch in a café not far from his brother's headquarters because I wanted to call in afterwards to see him. He would be off duty at two o'clock, he said on the telephone; if that would do, he could see me before he went home.

Erik spent most of lunch explaining with chapter and verse why all revolutions ended in gloom because all revolutionaries were incapable of humour.

'If the activists knew how to be funny,' he said, 'the workers would have ruled the world long ago.'

'Jokes should be taught in school,' I suggested.

He looked at me suspiciously. 'Are you taking the micky?'

'I thought that was the point.'

'Oh God, yes.' He laughed. 'So it is. What makes you spend your life detecting?'

'Curiosity.'

'Killed the cat.'

'Shut up.'

'Sorry,' he said, grinning. 'Anyway, you're still alive. How did you train for it? Is there a school for detectives?'

'Don't think so. I went to university. Tried industry, didn't like it. Didn't want to teach. Liked going racing . . . so got a job going racing.'

'That's as smart a canter over the course as I've ever heard, and as a gossip columnist I've heard a lot. What did you read at which university?'

'Psychology at Cambridge.'

'Ah-hah,' he said. 'Ah absolutely *Hah*.'

He came with me up to Knut's office, leaving Odin

in charge of the car. Knut was tired after an apparently frustrating spell of duty, yawning and rubbing his eyes when we walked in.

'I am sorry,' he said. 'But I have been awake since two o'clock this morning.' He shook his head to clear it. 'Never mind. How can I help you?'

'Not in detail today. Tell me if your terms of reference would let you catch a rabbit if I enticed one out of a hole.' I turned to Erik. 'Explain to him. If I set a trap, can he help me to spring it? Is he allowed to, and would he personally want to?'

The brothers consulted in their own language, Knut neat, restrained, over-tired, and Erik with undisciplined gestures, bohemian clothes and wild, wispy hair. Erik was older, but in him the life force still flowed with generous vigour.

In the end they both nodded. Knut said, 'As long as it is not against the regulations, I will help.'

'I'm very grateful.'

He smiled faintly. 'You are doing my work.'

He collected his coat and cap and came down to the street with us. His car, it appeared, was along with Erik's in the side road running down beside a small railed public garden.

Erik's car was a centre of attention.

About ten feet away from it, ranged round in a semi-circle, stood about a dozen children and one uncertain looking policeman. His face changed thankfully at the sight of Knut, and he saluted and began to shift his anxiety on to someone else.

Erik translated for me, looking puzzled.

'One of the children says a man told her not on any account to go near my car. He told her to run home as fast as she could.'

I looked at the car. Odin was not facing out of the front window as usual, but out of the back and he was looking down, not interestedly at the crowd. Something in the great dog's world seemed wrong to him. He was standing rigidly. Much too tense. And the boot was no longer tied up with string.

'Oh Christ,' I said. 'Get those children out of here. Make them run.'

They simply stared at me and didn't move. But they hadn't been near the Old Bailey in London on 8 March 1973.

'It could be a bomb,' I said.

CHAPTER TWELVE

The children recognized the word but of course they didn't believe it. The people in London hadn't believed it until the flying glass ripped their faces.

'Tell them to run,' I said to Knut.

He decided to take it seriously, even if it were a false alarm. He said something unequivocal to the policeman, and he grabbed hold of Erik's arm.

He knew his brother. He must have loved him more than most. He grabbed him tight just as Erik took his first step towards the car, saying 'Odin,' half under his breath.

They more or less fought. Knut wouldn't let go and Erik grew frantic. Knut put a lock on Erik's arm which would have arrested a twenty stone boxer with a skinful, and Erik's face crumpled into despair. The two of them, step by contested step, retreated from the car.

The policeman had chased the children away to a safe distance and was yelling to approaching pedestrians to get behind cover. No one paid any attention to me, so I nipped smartly along the pavement, put my hand on the handle, wrenched the door open, and sprinted.

Even then the wretched dog didn't come out at once. It took a screeching whistle from Erik to get results, and Odin came bounding after me down the pavement as if it were playtime.

The bomb went off just as he drew level, twenty feet from the car. The blast slammed us both down in a heap, hitting like a fierce blow in the back, knocking all breath out, leaving one limp, weak, and shaken.

Not a big bomb by Irish standards. But this one had presumably not been meant to destroy the neighbourhood. Just the occupants of a car. Two men and a dog.

Knut helped me to my feet and Erik took hold of Odin's collar, kneeling down and patting him solicitously. Odin slobbered all over him, as good as new.

'That was stupid,' Knut said.

'Yes,' I said.

'Are you hurt?'

'No.'

'You deserve to be.'

'It might not have gone off for hours.'

'It might have gone off while you were beside it.'

Erik's car was gutted. Windows blown out, interior torn to shreds, boot burst wide open. I picked splinters of glass out of the hair on the back of my head and asked him if it was insured.

'I don't know,' he said vaguely. He rubbed his arm where Knut had locked it. 'Knut wanted me to wait for an expert to come to see if it was a bomb, and if it was, to dismantle it.'

'Knut was quite right.'

'He didn't stop you.'

'I'm not his brother. He had his hands full with you, and the bomb probably had my name on it in the first place.'

'What a bloody awful way to die.' He stood up and grinned suddenly, his whole face lighting up. 'Thanks anyway,' he said. Which was pretty generous, considering the state of his Volvo.

Once the fireworks were over the children came back, staring at the wreck with wide eyes. I asked Knut to find the little girl who'd been told to run home, and he said he'd already sent his policeman to bring her.

Apart from the car, there was little damage. The windows had been broken in a severe-looking building on the far side of the road, but neither the railings nor the shivering bushes in the little public garden nearest the Volvo seemed to have suffered. Cars parked several yards away fore and aft were slightly scratched with glass splinters but otherwise undamaged. If the bomb had gone off while we had been driving along a busy street, there would have been a lot more mess.

The little girl was blonde, solemn, hooded and zipped into a red anorak, and accompanied now by a scolding older child of about thirteen who had fallen down on the job of looking after her and was busy justifying herself. Knut, as with the boy on the racecourse, won the smaller girl's confidence by squatting down to her level and chatting along quietly.

I leant against the railings and felt cold, and watched Erik smoothing Odin's sand-coloured skin over and over, seeing him dissipate an overwhelming build-up of tension in small, self-controlled gestures. Odin himself seemed to be enjoying it.

Knut stood up, holding the little girl's hand.

'Her name is Liv. She is four. She lives about half a mile away and she was playing in the park with her big sister. She came out of the gate down there and walked up the road here. Her sister had told her not to, but Liv says she doesn't do what her sister says.'

'The sister's too damn bossy,' Erik said unexpectedly. 'Little Fascist.'

'Liv says there was a man cutting some string at the back of the car and the big dog looking at him out of the window. She stopped to watch. She was behind the man. He didn't see her or hear her. She says he took something out of his coat and put it inside the boot, but she didn't see what shape it was. She says the man tried to shut the back of the car, but it wouldn't shut. Then he tried to tie the string where it had been before, but it was too short because he had cut it. He put the string in his pocket, and that was when he saw Liv. He told her to go away, but she seems to be a child who does the opposite of what she's told. She says she went up to the car and looked through the side window at the dog, but the dog went on looking out of the back.

Then the man shook her and told her to run home at once and not to play near the car. Then he went away.'

Knut looked at the small crowd of children beginning to cluster again round Liv.

'She is one of those children who draws others to her. Like now. They came out of the park to join her, and she told them about the man cutting the string and trying to tie the boot shut again. It was that which interested her most, it seemed. Then my policeman came along, on his way to start his afternoon duty, and he asked the children why they were standing there.'

'Then we came?'

'Right.'

'Has Liv said what the man looked like?'

'Big, she said. But all men are big to little girls.'

'Could she see his hair?'

Knut asked her. She answered. Knut said, 'He was wearing a woollen cap, like a sailor.'

'What did his eyes look like?'

Knut asked. Her little voice rose clear, high, definite, and all the children looked interested.

'He had yellow eyes. Sharp, like a bird.'

'Did he have gloves?'

Knut asked. 'Yes,' he reported.

'What sort of shoes?'

Back came the answer: big, soft, squashy shoes, like on a boat.

Children were the best witnesses on earth. Their eyes saw clearly, their memories were accurate, and their impressions weren't interpreted by probability or prejudice. So when Liv added something which made Knut and Erik and the older children laugh, I asked what she'd said.

'She must have been mistaken,' Knut said.

'What did she say?'

'She said he had a butterfly on his neck.'

'Ask her what sort of butterfly,' I said.

'It's too late for butterflies,' Knut said patiently. 'Too cold.'

'Ask her what it was like,' I urged.

He shrugged, but he asked. The reply surprised him, because Liv described it with sharp positive little nods. She knew she'd seen a butterfly.

Knut said, 'She says it was on the back of his neck. She saw it because his head was bent forward. It was between his woolly cap and his collar and it didn't move.'

'What colour?'

He consulted. 'Dark red.'

'Birth mark?'

'Could be,' he agreed. He asked her one or two more questions and nodded to me. 'I should think so,' he said. 'She says it had two wings lying open flat, but one was bigger than the other.'

'So all we need now is a big man with yellow eyes and a butterfly birthmark.'

'Or a small man,' Erik said, 'With the sun in his eyes and a dirty neck.'

'No sun,' I said. The iron grey sky pressed down like an army blanket, without warmth. The shivers in my gut, however, had little to do with the cold.

Knut sent his policeman to fetch experts in finger-prints and explosives and took the names and addresses of half the children. The crowd of watchers grew a bit, and Erik restively asked Knut when he could go home.

'What in?' said Knut pointedly, so we stamped around on the pavement for nearly another hour.

With darkness we returned to Knut's office. He took his coat and cap off and looked wearier than ever.

I borrowed his telephone and rang the Sandviks to apologize for my non-arrival. I spoke, in the event, to Mrs Per Bjørn, who explained that her husband was out.

'Mikkel did wait for you, Mr Cleveland,' she said in heavily accented English. 'But after one hour he went away with some friends.'

'Please tell him I'm very sorry.'

'I will tell him.'

'What school does he go to?'

'College of Gol,' she said, and then thought better of it. 'But I do not think that my husband would like . . .'

I interrupted, 'I just wondered if I could see him this evening before he goes back.'

'Oh . . . He is going straight back with the friends. They will have started by now.'

'Never mind, then.'

I put down the receiver. Knut was organizing coffee.

'Where is the College of Gol?' I asked.

'Gol is in the mountains, on the way to Bergen. It is a holiday ski town, in the winter. The college is a boarding school for rich boys. Are you going all the way out there to see Mikkel Sandvik? He knows nothing about Bob Sherman's death. When I saw him he was very upset about his friend dying like that. He would have helped me if he could.'

'How upset? Crying?'

'No, not crying. Pale. Very shocked. Trembling. *Upset*.'

'Angry?'

'No. Why should he be angry?'

'People are usually furious when their friends are murdered. They feel like strangling the murderer, don't they?'

'Oh, that,' he said, nodding. 'No, I don't remember that Mikkel was especially angry.'

'What is he like?' I asked.

'Just a boy. Sixteen. No, seventeen. Intelligent, but not outstanding. Average height, slim build, light brown hair, good manners. Nothing unusual about him. A nice boy. A little nervous, perhaps.'

We sat around and drank the coffee. Odin had some too, in a bowl, with a lot of sugar. Erik had recovered from the nearness of losing his companion and was beginning to think about his car.

'I'll need to hire one, I suppose,' he said. 'For driving David around.'

187

'You're not driving David any more,' Knut said positively.

'Of course I am.'

'No,' said Knut. 'It's too dangerous.'

There was a small meaningful silence. Anyone in future who drove me must be presumed to be at risk. Which put me high in the unpopularity stakes as a passenger.

'I'll manage,' I said.

Erik said, 'Where do you plan to go?'

'Tomorrow, to call on Sven Wangen, then to Øvrevoll. On Monday . . . I don't know yet.'

'I could do with another of those Grand breakfasts,' he said.

'No,' said Knut. They argued heatedly in private, and Knut lost. He turned a grim face and a compressed mouth to me. 'Erik says he never leaves a job unfinished.'

Erik grinned and rubbed a hand over his straggly blond hair. 'Only dull ones.'

Knut said crossly, 'I suppose you realize that one of these attempts will be successful? Two have failed, but . . .'

'Three,' I said. 'Someone tried to drown me in the fjord the first day I came to Norway.'

I told them about the black speedboat. Knut frowned and said, 'But that could have been an accident.'

I nodded. 'At the time, I thought it was. I don't think

188

so any longer.' I got up to pour myself some more hot strong black coffee. 'I do rather agree with you that they will succeed in the end, but I don't know what to do about it.'

'Give up and go back to England,' Knut said.

'Would you?'

He didn't answer. Nor did Erik. There wasn't an answer to give.

Knut sent me back in a police car to the Grand, where as the bar was again shut (Saturday) I ate an early dinner, collected my suitcases and Bob Sherman's helmet from the porter, picked a room at random from those available, and spent the evening upstairs alone, sitting in an armchair and contemplating several unpalatable facts.

Such as, there was a limit to luck and little girls.

Such as, next time they could use a rifle, because sniping was the surest way of killing.

Such as, tomorrow if I went to the races I would be scared to death the whole bloody day.

Not much comfort in the hope that old yellow eyes with the birthmark might be a lousy shot.

There were various other thoughts, chiefly that somewhere there existed a particular way of discovering who had killed Bob Sherman, and why. There had to be such a way, for if there wasn't, no one would need to kill me. Knut hadn't found it. Maybe he had looked the solution in the face and not recognized it, which was easy enough to do. Maybe I had, also, but could be expected to understand later what I had heard or seen.

Yellow eyes must have followed Erik's car, I thought. Erik's breakneck driving and red light jumping made it exceedingly unlikely that anything bar a fire engine could have tailed us to Øvrevoll: but then I'd considerately returned to the Grand to dump the helmet, and made it easy for a watcher to pick us up again.

I hadn't spotted a follower, nor had Erik. But our trip to Baltzersen's and from there to where we parked for lunch had been comparatively short and, in retrospect, almost legal. Anyone risking a couple of head-on crashes could have kept us in sight.

Yellow eyes was the man who had attacked Emma; and it seemed likely that the man who kicked her grandfather was the man who'd tried to knife me. Both, it seemed to me, were mercenaries, paid to do a violent job but not the instigators. They hadn't the aura of principals.

To my mind there were at least two others, one of whom I knew, one or more I didn't. To bring out the unknown, I had to bamboozle the known. The big snag was that when it came to setting traps, the only bait at present available was myself, and this cheese could find itself eaten if it wasn't extremely careful.

It was easy to see that to bring out the big boys, yellow eyes and brown eyes would have to be decoyed away while at the same time a situation needing instant action was temptingly arranged elsewhere. How to do it was another matter. I stared at the carpet for ages and came up with nothing foolproof.

I wished there was a way of knowing what Bob Sherman had been bringing to Norway. Unlikely to be straight pornography, because Bob had told Paddy O'Flaherty that he, Bob, had been conned. If he had opened the packet and found that it did not contain ordinary pornography, he might well have thought that.

Suppose . . . he had opened the packet and reckoned he was not being paid enough for what he was carrying.

Suppose . . . he had removed something from the packet, meaning to use it to up the stakes.

But . . . he couldn't have used it, because, if he had, the enemy would have known he had taken it, and would not have killed him without getting it back.

So suppose . . . simply opening the packet and seeing the contents was in itself a death warrant.

Suppose . . . the enemy killed him for knowing the contents, and only discovered afterwards that he had removed some of them.

It came back to that every time.

So . . . what the *hell* was in that packet?

Start another way.

When had he opened the packet?

Probably not at home. Emma had seen him put it in

his overnight bag so as not to risk forgetting it. Yellow eyes and friend had subsequently smashed the place up looking for things from it, and hadn't found any. So it seemed reasonable to suppose that he had set off from home with the envelope intact.

He had had all day at Kempton races. Time enough if he'd urgently wanted to open it: but if he'd felt like that, he'd already had it available all night.

Not much time at Heathrow between arriving from Kempton and boarding the aeroplane. Hardly the opportunity for an impulsive bit of snooping.

He had turned up at Gunnar Holth's an hour or so later than expected. So he could have done his lethal bit of nosey-parkering either on the flight or in the first hour after he'd landed.

On the flight, I thought, was most likely of all.

A couple of drinks under his belt, an hour or so to while away, and a packet of blue pictures temptingly to hand.

Open the packet and see . . . what?

Suppose he had had perhaps half an hour before landing to come up with the idea of demanding a larger freight fee. Suppose he took something out of the envelope and hid it . . . where had he hidden it?

Not in his pockets or his overnight bag. Perhaps in his saddle, but doubtful, because for one thing his racing saddle was tiny, and for another he'd ridden three races on it the following day.

Not in his helmet: no papers or photographs lurked inside the padded headband.

Which left one unaccounted-for hour, during which he could have left any object at the reception desk of any hotel in Oslo, with a request to keep it for him until he returned.

In one hour he could have hidden something anywhere.

I sighed. It was hopeless.

I stood up, stretched, unpacked a few things, undressed, brushed my teeth.

Bob's helmet lay on my bed. I picked it up and dangled it by the chin strap as I pulled back the quilt and pushed up the pillows as a back-rest for reading before sleep. Sitting between the sheets I turned the helmet idly over in my hands, scarcely looking at it, thinking about Bob and the last day he'd worn it.

I thought seriously about wearing it myself to Øvrevoll to protect my head, and buying a bullet-proof vest besides. I thought ungenerous thoughts about Emma's husband because I too could still die for what he'd done.

No papers. No photographs. I pulled the soft black padding out again. Nothing, still nothing tucked behind it.

In the crown there was just the small round centre-piece of black-covered padding suspended by straps fixed into the shell itself. A marvellous piece of engin-eering, designed to prevent a man falling on his nut at thirty miles an hour off a galloping horse from bashing his skull in. The central suspended piece of padding shielded the top of the head and stopped it crashing into the shell itself at concussion speed.

Underneath the central piece of padding there was no room at all for any papers or photographs or anything out of magazine-sized packets. I put my hand below it, just to make sure.

And there, in the roof of his helmet, Bob had left the key.

Literally, the key.

I felt it there with complete disbelief.

Fixed to the hard outer casing by two crossed strips of sellotape, unseen until one deliberately pushed the central piece of padding sideways out of position, was a key.

I unstuck it from the helmet and pulled off the sticky tape. It was a yale-type key, but with a small black tag bonded on instead of the usual round metal thumb plate. A small white number, C14, was stamped on the black plastic on the side which had been against the helmet's wall. The key itself, at first, second, third glance, had been unnoticeable: and Bob certainly could have ridden his races with it firmly and invisibly in place.

C14.

It looked like a locker key. Very like those from the left-luggage lockers of any big airport or railway station in the world. Nothing at all to show to which city, country or continent it belonged.

I thought.

If the key had been in the package, one would have expected it to be of extreme importance. Vital enough to be worth dragging the pond for, when it was found to be missing. Or searching for at once in the house in England.

The men searching the house in England had specifically mentioned papers. They had been looking for papers, not a key.

So, suppose Bob had left the papers somewhere in a locker, and this was the key to it.

Much easier. It cut out New York, Nairobi and outer Mongolia and narrowed the search to most of southern England or anywhere in Oslo.

The harmless-looking little key promised to be everything I needed. I closed my hand over it, with an illogical instinct to hide it, to keep it safe.

Bob too must have felt like that. The care with which he'd hidden it revealed the strength of his instinct. And he hadn't known at the time how true that instinct had been.

Smiling at myself I nevertheless followed his example.

There was in my suitcase a fresh unopened dressing for the cut on my chest, thoughtfully provided by Charles Stirling in case I needed it: but since the intermittent throbbing had faded to an intermittent itch, I'd left his original handiwork undisturbed.

Laying the key on the bedside table I pulled off the old dressing to take a look: and dark, dry and healthy, the slit was healing fast.

I fetched the new plaster and stuck it on, with Bob Sherman's precious key snug inside it against my skin.

CHAPTER THIRTEEN

Erik came to breakfast looking almost as depressed as the freezing wet day outside. He brought two plates heaped like the Matterhorn over from the buffet, sat opposite me, and toyed with the foothills.

'Did you sleep well?' he asked.

'No.'

'Nor did I. Kept hearing the bang of that bloody bomb.' He looked at the smoked fish I had acquired before his arrival. 'Aren't you eating?'

'Not madly hungry.'

He raised a grin. 'The condemned man syndrome?'

'Thanks.'

He sighed, adjusted his mind to the task and began proving his stomach was as big as his eyes. When both plates were empty of all but a trace of oil and six dorsal fins he patted his mouth with a napkin and resurfaced to the dangerous Sunday.

'Are you seriously going to the races?' he said.

'Don't know yet.'

'I didn't bring Odin today. Left him with a

neighbour.' He drank his coffee. 'I hired a bigger Volvo. A fast one. Here's the bill.' He dug in his pocket and produced a receipt.

I took out my wallet and paid him. He didn't say leave it until later.

A party of English racing people came into the restaurant in ones and twos and sat together at a table near the window. I knew most of them: a top amateur jump rider, a pro from the flat, an assistant trainer, an owner and his wife. When they'd chosen their food and begun to eat I drifted over to them and pulled up a chair.

'Hi,' they said. 'How's things?'

Things, meaning mostly their chances that afternoon, were relaxedly discussed, and after a while I asked the question I had joined them for.

'Remember the weekend Bob Sherman disappeared? Did any of you happen to come over with him on the same flight?'

The top amateur rider had. Glory be.

'Did you sit next to each other?'

He explained delicately that he had travelled first class, Bob tourist.

'But,' he said, 'I gave him a lift into Oslo in my taxi.'

'Where did you drop him?'

'Oh . . . here. I was staying here, but he was going on to that trainer feller he rode for. He thanked me for the ride . . . and I think he said he would catch the Lijordet tram if there was one. Anyway, I remember him standing on the pavement with his bag and saddle and stuff. But does it matter? After all, he rode next day, all right.'

'Was the flight on time?'

'Don't remember that it wasn't.'

I asked a few more questions, but the amateur remembered nothing else of much significance.

'Thanks anyway,' I said.

'Hope you get whoever did it,' he said. He smiled. 'I expect you will.'

If he didn't get me, I thought with a twinge, and went back to collect Erik.

'Where first?'

'All the railway stations.'

'All the *what*?'

'The nearest railway station,' I amended.

'Whatever for?'

'I want a time-table.'

'They have them here at the hotel desk.'

I grinned at him. 'Which is the nearest station?'

He said doubtfully, 'The Østbanen, I suppose.'

'Off we go, then.'

He shook his head in exasperation, but off we went.

From the Østbanen, I discovered, trains ran through Gol on the line to Bergen. Trains ran also to Lille-hammer, Trondheim, and the Arctic circle. Østbanen was the main long-distance terminus in Oslo.

It had left-luggage lockers and it even had a C14.

But the locker was empty, the key was in the open door, and the tag was different.

I took time-tables which included Gol, where Mikkel Sandvik's school was.

One never knew.

'What now?' Erik said.

'The other railway stations,' I said, and we went there, but without finding any matching black tags.

'Where else would you find lockers like those?'

'Besides railway stations? At the airport. In factories, offices, schools. Lots of places.'

'Available to a foreign traveller at eight-thirty on a Saturday evening.'

'Ah . . . Fornebu. Where else?' Where else indeed. 'Shall we go there?'

'Later,' I said. 'After Sven Wangen.'

Erik objected. 'He lives in the opposite direction, further out than the racecourse.'

'All the same,' I said. 'Sven Wangen first.'

'You're the boss.'

He looked carefully several times in the driving mirror as we set off, but said he was sure we were not being followed. I believed him. Nothing could have stayed with Erik when he was really trying.

'Tell me about Sven Wangen,' I said.

He pursed his mouth in much the same disapproving way that Arne had.

'His father was a collaborator,' he said.

'And no one forgets it?'

He sniffed. 'Officially, the past is past. But after the war, the collaborators didn't thrive. If some town wanted a bridge built or a school, for instance, it would happen that an architect or a builder who had worked well with the Nazis would just not be the one to get the contract.'

'But Sven Wangen's father was already rich . . . from shipping.'

He looked at me sideways while taking a sharp turn to the left and missed a lamp post by millimetres.

'Arne Kristiansen told me,' I said.

'Inherited wealth is immoral,' Erik said. 'All estates should be distributed among the masses.'

'Especially the estates of collaborators?'

He grinned. 'I suppose so.'

'Was the father like the son?' I asked.

Erik shook his head. 'A hard-headed greedy businessman. He made a lot of money out of the Nazis.'

'Surely that was patriotic of him?'

Erik wouldn't have it. 'He did nothing for his fellow-countrymen. He made money only for himself.'

'The father destroyed the son,' I said.

'Destroyed him?' He shook his head. 'Sven Wangen is an overpowering boor who always gets his way. He's nowhere near destroyed.'

'He's an empty person. Because of his father, I shouldn't think he ever had a chance to be normally liked, and people who are spurned for no fault of their own can become terribly aggressive.'

He thought it over. 'Guess you may be right. But I still don't like him.'

Sven Wangen lived in the style to which he had been born in a huge country house built mostly of wood, partly of stone. Even on a cold wet early winter morning it looked neat, clean and prosperous. Everything growing was sharply clipped into geometric precision, a regimentation totally uncongenial to Erik's casual, generous and untidy mind. He stared around in distaste, his give-everything-to-the-masses expression much in evidence.

'All this for two people,' he said. 'It's wrong.'

The place oppressed me as well, but for a different reason. There were too many windows all looking with black eyes towards the car. If I got out and stood away from its protection I would be a sitting target for anyone in that house with a gun.

Erik got out of the car. I had to force myself to follow him.

And of course, no one shot. If I'd really thought they would I wouldn't have gone. But it was one thing telling myself that Sven Wangen wasn't going to kill me on his own doorstep and another getting my nerves to believe it. Something, I thought grimly, was going to have to be done about those stupid nerves, or I'd never complete the course.

A middle-aged woman came to open the front door and show me down the hall to a small sitting-room with windows facing the drive. Through them I could see

Erik pacing up and down in the rain radiating Marxist disapproval and stamping the undeserving bourgeoisie into the gravel with each crunch of his heel.

Sven Wangen strolled into the room eating a sugary pastry and staring with cold eyes down from a great height.

'I'd forgotten you were coming,' he said. 'Have you solved everything yet?' A slight sneer. No friendliness.

'Not everything.'

A small bad-tempered flash in the supercilious eyes.

'I've nothing to tell you. You are wasting your time.'

They'd all told me that, and they were all mistaken.

Without a hat, Sven Wangen was revealed as going prematurely bald, the russet hair as thick as ever round the back and sides, but almost as thin as Erik's on top. He took a large sticky bite, chewed, swallowed: added another fraction to his overweight.

'The last day Bob Sherman rode for you, did he say anything unexpected?'

'No, he did not.' He hadn't bothered to think about it.

'Did you take him for a drink to celebrate the winner he rode for you?'

'Certainly not.' He started another mouthful.

'Did you talk to him at all . . . either before or after the race?'

He chewed. Swallowed. Looked closely at the pastry, prospecting the next area.

'In the parade ring, I gave him his orders. I told him

I expected better than he'd just done for Rolf Torp. He said he understood.'

Bite. Munch. Swallow.

'After the race, he unsaddled the horse and went to weigh in. I didn't see him again.'

'While he was unsaddling, did he tell you how the mare had run?'

'No. I was telling Holth she needed a good thrashing to quieten her down. Holth disagreed. I didn't speak to Sherman.'

'Didn't you congratulate him?' I asked curiously.

'No.'

'Do you wish you had?'

'Why should I?'

You might need to eat less, I thought, but refrained from saying so. His psychological hang-ups weren't in this instance my affair.

'Did he mention delivering a package which he had brought from England?'

'No.' He stuffed the rest of the gooey goody into his mouth and had difficulty closing his lips.

'Did you ask him to ride the mare next time he came?'

He stared, then spoke round the dough and currants. 'He didn't come again.'

'I mean, that last day, did you ask him to ride for you again?'

'Oh. No.' He shrugged. 'Holth always engages the jockeys. I just say who I want.'

'You never telephoned to Sherman in England personally to discuss his rides for you?'

'Certainly not.'

'Some owners do talk to their jockeys,' I said.

'I pay Holth to do that sort of thing.'

What a lot you miss, I thought. Poor fat unloved deprived rich young man. I thanked him for his time and went back to Erik. Sven Wangen watched us through the window, licking the sugar off his fingers.

'Well?' Erik said.

'He might have issued the orders, but he never killed anyone himself.'

Erik grunted as he started the hired Volvo towards the gate. 'Where now?'

'You're wet,' I said. 'Why did you stay out in the rain?'

He was almost embarrassed. 'Oh . . . I thought I'd hear you better if you yelled.'

We went in silence for five miles down the road and then he pulled up at a fork.

'You'll have to decide here,' he said. 'That way to Øvrevoll, and that way to the airport. The racecourse is much nearer.'

'The airport.'

'Right.'

He blasted off down the road to Fornebu as if trying to fly there.

'Mind we aren't followed,' I said.

'You're joking.'

The thirty mile journey, from one side of Oslo to the other, took just over half an hour.

No one followed.

C14 was locked and C13 next to it had a key in its door with a black tag, just the same. Both were large lockers in the bottom row of a three-high tier.

Erik, who had allotted himself full bodyguard status, stood at my elbow and peered at the ranks of metal doors.

'Are these the lot you're looking for?'

I nodded. 'I think so.'

'What do we do now, then?'

'We walk around for a bit to make sure there's no one here we know.'

'A sensible idea.'

We walked around and stood in corners to watch, but as far as I could see every person in the airport was a complete stranger. Drifting gently back to the lockers, Erik stood stalwartly with his back to C13 and looked ready to repel boarders while I inconspicuously fished out the hidden key and tried it in the lock next door.

The right key, no mistake. The locker door swung open revealing a space big enough for two large suitcases: and on the scratched metal floor, looking lost and inappropriate, lay a folded piece of paper.

I bent down, picked it up, and tucked it into my inside jacket pocket.

'See anyone?' I asked Erik, straightening again.

'Not a soul we know.'

'Let's grab some coffee.'

'What about the locker?'

I looked down at C14 with its key in the lock and its door open.

'We don't need it any more.'

Erik steered us to the airport buffet and bought coffee for both of us and a couple of open sandwiches for himself. We sat at a plastic-topped table amid travellers with untidy hand luggage and children running about doing what they were told not to, and with an almost fluttery feeling of expectation I took out the paper Bob Sherman had left.

I had supposed it would prove to be a base for blackmail: incriminating letters or photographs no one dared show his wife. But it proved to be neither of those things. It proved to be something I didn't recognize at all.

For one thing, the paper was thinner than I had at first supposed, and only seemed to be thick because it was folded several times. Unfolded, it turned out to be a strip six inches across but nearly three feet long, and it was divided into three columns which were intended to be read downwards. One could not, however, actually read them, as each inch and a half wide column seemed to be composed of variously shaded blocks and squares, not letters or figures. Down the long left-hand edge of the paper were numbers at regular intervals, starting with 3 at the top and ending with 14 at the bottom. Across the top in hand-written capitals was a single heading: Data Summary.

I refolded the strip and put it back in my pocket.

'What is it?' Erik asked.

I shook my head. 'Don't know.'

He stirred his coffee. 'Knut will find out.'

I considered that and didn't especially like it.

'No,' I said. 'This paper came from England. I think I'll take it back there to find out what it is.'

'It's Knut's case,' he said with a certain amount of quiet obstinacy.

'Mine as well.' I hesitated. 'Tell Knut I found the paper if you must, but I'd rather you didn't mention it to anyone at all. I don't want it leaking out round Oslo, and if you tell Knut he will have to record it, and if he records it, you never know who will see it. I'd much rather tell him myself when I get back. We can't anyway make a useful plan of campaign until we know what we're dealing with, so nothing can really be gained by telling him now.'

He looked unconvinced, but after a while all he said was, 'Where did you find the key to the locker?'

'In Bob Sherman's helmet.'

His obstinacy slowly melted to resignation.

'All right,' he said. 'I won't tell Knut. He could have found the key first.'

As logic it hardly stood up, but I was grateful. I looked at my watch and said, 'I can catch the two five to Heathrow.'

'Right now?' He sounded surprised.

I nodded. 'Don't tell anyone I've gone. I don't want any friend of yellow eyes waiting at the other end.'

He grinned. 'David Cleveland? Who's he?' He stood up and turned to go. 'I'll give your regards to Odin.'

I watched his untidy back depart forthwith through the scattered crowd towards the distant exit and felt unexpectedly vulnerable without him. But nothing dire happened. I caught the flight and landed safely at Heathrow, and, after thought, left my car where it was in the car park and took myself by train to Cambridge.

Sunday evening in mid-term was as good a time as any to beard professors in their dens, but the first one I backed was a loser. He lectured in Computer Science: but my Data Summary, he said, had nothing to do with computers. Why didn't I try Economics? I tried Economics who said why didn't I try Geology.

Although it was by then getting on for ten o'clock I tried Geology, who took one brief glance at the paper and said, 'Christ, where did you get this, they guard these things like gold dust.'

'What is it?' I asked.

'A core. A chart of a core. From a drilling. See those numbers down the left-hand side? I'd say they refer to the depth of each section. Might be in hundreds of feet. Might be in thousands.'

'Can you tell where the drilling was done?'

He shook his head, a youngish earnest man with a mass of reddish hair merging into an undisciplined beard.

'Could be anywhere in the world. You'd need the key to the shadings even to guess what they were looking for.'

I said in depression, 'Isn't there any way of finding out where it came from?'

'Oh Lord, yes,' he said cheerfully. 'Depends how important it is.'

'It's a long story,' I said doubtfully, with a look at his clock.

'Sleep is a waste of time,' he said like a true scholar, so I told him more or less exactly why I wanted to know.

'Have a beer?' he suggested, when I'd finished.

'Thanks.'

He found two cans under a heap of uncorrected essays and ripped off the rings.

'Cheers!' he said, dispensing with a glass. 'All right. You convinced me. I'll pass you on to the people who drew that chart.'

I was astonished. 'How do you know who drew it?'

He laughed. 'It's like knowing a colleague's handwriting. Any research geologist could probably tell you where that chart came from. It's a research lab job. I'll give the managing director a ring in the morning and explain, and see if he'll help you. They're awfully touchy about these charts.' He eyed it thoughtfully. 'I shouldn't be surprised if there'll be an unholy row, because from what you've said I should think it was stolen.'

The seeds of the unholy row were plain to see, next day, on the face of Dr William Leeds, managing director of the Wessex-Wells Research Laboratory. An impressive man, small, calm and decisive, he looked deeply disturbed at what I'd brought him.

'Sit down, Mr Cleveland,' he said.

We sat one each side of his managerial desk.

'Tell me where you got this.'

I told him. He listened intently, without interrupting. At the end he said, 'What do you want to know?'

'What this chart is about. Who could benefit from getting hold of it, and how.'

He smiled. 'Fairly comprehensive.' He looked out of his big first floor office window for a while at a row of leaf-dropping willows across a stretch of lawn. Deep in the heart of Dorset, the laboratory stood in ancient parkland, a Victorian country residence sitting easily beside new low flat-topped workaday workshops. Dr Leeds's window overlooked the main artery of pathways linking the complex, a neat finger on the pulse if ever I saw one.

'Almost anyone could benefit from getting hold of

it,' he said. 'If they were unscrupulous. This chart cost perhaps half a million pounds.'

My mouth fell open. He laughed.

'Well . . . you have to remember that drill rigs are enormously sophisticated and expensive. You don't get a core by digging a hole with a spade. This one . . .' he tapped the paper, 'is only five inches in diameter but about fourteen thousand feet in depth. A fourteen thousand foot drilling costs a lot of money.'

'I can see,' I said, 'that it does.'

'Of course you couldn't sell it for that, but I should think this particular chart might be worth a hundred thousand, if you had a market.'

I asked if he would explain in more detail.

'A chart like this is information. You can always sell information illegally if you know someone ready to buy. Well . . . suppose this core showed a deposit of nickel, which it doesn't, incidentally, and you knew exactly from which particular drilling it came, you would know whether it was worth investing money in the drilling company, or not. For instance, during the Poseidon nickel boom in Australia, you'd have been able to make literally millions on the stock market through knowing infallibly in advance which of the dozens of prospecting companies had made the drilling that was richest in ore.'

'Good grief,' I said.

'It can work the other way too,' he said. 'If you know that a concession which has been expected to give a high yield is in fact not going to be good, you can sell out while the share price is still high.'

'So it wouldn't only be people engaged in mining who would be ready to buy such a chart.'

'Certainly not. The people who make most out of the earth probably don't know what a drill looks like.'

I said, 'Why sell the chart to someone else? Why not make millions on the stock market yourself?'

He smiled. 'It's much safer to be paid a lump sum into a nice anonymous Swiss bank account than to start dealing in shares. Any geologist dealing much in significant shares would be detected at once.'

'Do people approach geologists, asking them to sell information?'

'They do. We try to protect our geologists here by not letting them know exactly where the material they're working on has come from. But obviously we have not been entirely successful.' He looked bleak. 'We know from past experience that a working geologist is usually approached by a middle man, an entrepreneur who buys information from the research source and then sells it to a bigger fish who operates in the world markets.'

'Am I dealing with the middle man or the big fish?'

He smiled and shook his head. 'Can't tell. But the middle man, I suspect, as you found the chart so close to source.'

'What exactly do these columns mean?' I asked.

He picked up the chart and showed me. 'The first

column is lithology . . . the composition of the rock layers. The second is the original particle type . . . that means micro- and macrofossils and micrite. The third . . .' He compressed his lips, clearly most upset by this one. 'The third is a fairly new and highly secret process, scanning electron microscopy. Our clients will be particularly furious that this finding has been leaked. They paid a mint for it. We can stay in business here only as long as every client remains convinced that the analysis he is paying for will never be seen by anyone except himself.'

I said, 'This chart wouldn't be much use, though, without the key to the various shadings.'

'No.' He thought. 'If I had to guess, I'd say that this might be used as a sort of appetizer, or a proof that the middle man had the real goods to sell. We don't normally make up charts in this form. This is an abbreviation. A condensed, composite edition. Specially made.'

'But would the rest of Bob Sherman's package be worth anything without this chart?'

'Oh, sure. It depends what else was in it. A written analysis would be just as good as a chart. If they had a written analysis it wouldn't matter all that much if they lost the chart.'

I thanked him for his help. 'Could you tell me where that drilling was made . . . and what for?'

He glanced at it. 'I can tell you in general just by

looking at it. But do you want to know precisely, to the half mile?'

'Please,' I said.

'Then come with me.'

He led me along a wide passage, through some swing doors, and into a modern wing tacked on to the back of the original house. We were bound, it seemed, for the records department, but to get in there even the managing director had to announce himself to the inmates and get the door unlocked electronically from inside.

He smiled wryly at my surprise.

'We usually pride ourselves on our security. We're going to have a great upheaval sorting out which of our people sold the information on this chart.' A thought struck him. 'I suppose you wouldn't like to come back and work on it yourself?'

I wouldn't have minded, but explained about the Jockey Club.

'Pity,' he said.

He unerringly sorted out one particular folder from the thousands in the filing cupboards which lined the walls. He knew exactly which company had commissioned the analysis, and he knew roughly from where the core had been taken.

He turned a few pages, comparing the chart with the notes.

'There,' he said finally, pointing with his finger. 'Those are the coordinates you want.'

I looked over his arm. Read the coordinates.
Read the name of the company.
I'd never heard of it.
'Thank you very much,' I said.

CHAPTER FOURTEEN

I called to see Emma.

The cottage was warm and welcoming in the cold afternoon, alive with a glowing log fire and a huge vase of bronze chrysanthemums. None of the furniture had been replaced and the curtains were still at the cleaners, but Emma herself during the past week had made strides. There was at last a shade of colour in her cheeks and the faintest of sparkles in the eyes. The pretty girl had come back to life.

'David! How great to see you. Have a hot scone. They're just out of the oven.'

We sat in front of the fire eating the scones with butter and jam and concentration.

'Golly, you must have been hungry,' she said later, eyeing the almost-empty dish. 'I really made them to take over to Grandfather.' She laughed. 'Guess I'd better make some more.'

'They were lovely.' What with bombs and general

chasing around I had missed a lot of meals and picked at others. With Emma, for the first time in days, my stomach nerves felt safe enough to encourage intake.

'I don't know whether to ask,' she said, 'but have you found out anything about Bob?'

'Not enough.' I looked at my watch. 'May I use your telephone?'

'Of course.'

I called a stockbroker I knew who owned racehorses and asked him about the share movements of the company which had commissioned the analysis of the core.

'That's easy,' he said. 'About two months ago the share price started to soar. Someone had a hot tip, bought at the bottom and made a real packet.'

'Who?' I said.

'Impossible to tell, but probably a syndicate, considering the huge sums involved. All done through nominees, mostly on overseas markets.'

I thanked him and rang off; and after that I called SAS, who made warm noises and said sure there was a free seat on the six-thirty. A lot of my mind persisted in telling me that there was another flight in the morning and widows were meant for consoling: well, maybe, but not this one, not yet.

I kissed her goodbye.

'Come again,' she said, and I said, 'I will.'

*

I handed in at Heathrow the car I'd hired that morning in Cambridge, and squeezed into the six-thirty at the last call.

I didn't seem able to help the tension screwing up again as we began the descent into Oslo, but a harmless taxi took me uneventfully to the hotel, where the reception desk resignedly let me choose my own room.

I telephoned to Erik.

'Where are you?' he demanded.

'At the Grand.'

'For God's sake ... didn't you go?'

'There and back.'

'Did you find out ...?'

'Up to a point. I know what it is, but not who it belongs to. Look ... could you give me Knut's home number?'

He told me. 'Do you want any more driving done?'

'I'm afraid so, if you can face it.'

'Count,' he said, 'on me.'

I rang Knut who yawned and said he'd just come off duty and wouldn't be back until two o'clock the following afternoon.

'Do you know a place called Lillehammer?' I asked.

'*Ja*. Of course.'

'What's it like?'

'How do you mean? It is a big town. A tourist town in the summer, and a ski place in the winter. No visitors go there in October and November.'

'If you wanted to meet someone secretly in Lillehammer, within fairly easy walking distance of the railway station, where would you suggest?'

'Not in a public place?'

'No. Somewhere quiet.'

There was a pause. Then he said, 'It might be better to walk away from the town itself. Down towards the lake. There is a road going down to the bridge over the lake. It is the main road to Gjøvik, but there is not much traffic, and there are some small side roads down to the houses round the lakeside. Is that what you want?'

'Sounds perfect.'

'Who are you going to meet?'

I told him at considerable length. Somewhere along the way he shed his fatigue, because when he next spoke his voice was alert and even eager.

'Ja. I understand. I will arrange everything.'

'I'll see you in the morning, then.'

'Ja. Agreed. And . . . er . . . take good care, David.'

'You bet,' I said.

I rang Erik again, who said certainly he would come to breakfast, drive me to Knut's office, and get me to the station in time to catch the ten o'clock to Lillehammer.

'Is that all?'

'No . . . Would you meet me again when I get back? Four thirty, I think.'

'All right.' He sounded almost disappointed.

'Bring knuckledusters,' I said, which cheered him.

Next, Lars Baltzersen.

'Of course I've heard of that company,' he said. 'Their shares are booming. I bought some myself a few weeks ago and already they show a good profit.'

'Do you know anyone else who bought any while the price was still low?'

A pause, then he said, 'Rolf Torp did. I believe it was Rolf who told me about them, but I can't be sure.' He cleared his throat. 'I have heard worrying rumours, though, that the really big buyers were in the Middle East. One cannot be sure. There is much secrecy. But it seems likely.'

'Why would that be worrying?' I asked, and he told me.

Last of all I telephoned Arne. Kari answered, her voice warm, amused, and full of memory from our last meeting.

'Haven't seen you since Friday,' she said. 'Why don't you come to dinner here tomorrow?'

'Love to,' I said, 'but I don't think I can.'

'Oh. Well . . . how's the case going?'

'That's really what I wanted to talk about with Arne.'

She said she would fetch him, and he came on the line. He sounded glad that I'd called.

'David . . . haven't seen you for days,' he said. 'What have you been doing?'

'Ferreting,' I said. 'Look, Arne, I've had a piece of luck. Some man in a place called Lillehammer telephoned and said he could tell me something about Bob Sherman being killed. He said he almost saw it happen.

He wouldn't say any more on the phone, but I'm going to meet him tomorrow. The thing is . . . I wondered if you'd like to come with me. I'd be glad of your company, if you could spare the time. And he didn't speak very good English . . . so you could interpret for me, if you would.'

'Tomorrow?'

'Yes. I'm catching the ten o'clock train in the morning.'

'Where in Lillehammer are you meeting this man?'

'On the road to Gjøvik, down near the bridge over the lake. He's going to be there at midday.'

He said doubtfully, 'I suppose I could . . .'

'Please do come, Arne,' I said.

He made up his mind. '*Ja*. I'll come. Are you still staying at the Grand?'

'Yes,' I said. 'But you are nearer the station. I'll meet you there.'

'Right.' He hesitated again. 'I hope he isn't some lunatic, making up stories.'

'So do I,' I said.

I slept with my bed pushed right across the door, but nobody tried to get in.

Erik had brought Odin again to assist with the guard duty, although I now knew from longer acquaintance that the Dane's fierce appearance was only a front. A right great softy lived inside the sandy skin.

Together nonetheless they conveyed me safely to the police station where Knut met us, keenly awake a good five hours before he was due on duty. Up in his office I gave him the geological chart, which he inspected curiously.

'Don't lose it,' I said.

He smiled. 'Better to lose my life, I suspect.'

'You'll get it photo-copied?'

He nodded. 'Straight away.'

'See you this evening, then.'

We shook hands.

'Be careful,' he said.

Erik and Odin stuck beside me while I bought my ticket and walked to the barrier. It was the worst morning yet for jumpy nerves, with me far outstripping Arne in the matter of looking over my shoulder. By this evening, I thought grimly, I'd either be safe or dead. It seemed an awful long time to the evening.

Arne, already waiting on the platform, greeted me with a big smile.

'What number is your ticket?' he asked.

I hadn't realized that each ticket bore a seat number on the train, but it was so.

'I'll see if I can change mine to be next to you,' he said, and vanished on his errand at high speed. While he was gone I found my allotted number, a window seat facing forward, halfway up one of the large, airy coaches. With only a few minutes to go to departure time about half the seats were filled with respectable-looking citizens, and I managed to look over my shoulder only twice.

Arne returned with an air of satisfaction and the ticket for the seat beside mine.

'That's better,' he said, and gave all the worthy fellow travellers a severe inspection before sitting down. 'I should have waited for you at the ticket office . . . didn't think of it in time.'

Erik, with Odin still beside him, suddenly appeared on the platform outside the window, rapping to attract my attention and vigorously beckoning me to talk to him. I pointed to the rear of the carriage, excused myself past Arne, and went to the door to hear what Erik wanted to tell.

'I saw him,' he said, almost stuttering with urgency. 'Get off the train and come with me.'

'Who?'

'It'll go if you don't get off quickly. The man who planted the bomb. Big, with a butterfly birth-mark. I saw it. He was buying a ticket . . . he dropped some change and bent to pick it up. I saw his neck . . . and I saw his eyes. They really are a sort of yellow. Very light and bright and odd. Do hurry, David. There was another man with him. They got on this train, in the rear carriage. Three carriages back from here.'

A whistle blew. He practically danced with frustration.

'Get off. Get off . . .'

I shook my head. 'I'll find a way of avoiding them.' The train began to move. 'Thanks a lot. See you this afternoon. Mind you come.'

'Of course I'll come.'

The train gathered speed, diminishing my protectors second by second until I could no longer see the bewilderment on Erik's face or the patient lack of comprehension on Odin's.

'Who was that?' Arne asked as I returned to my place.

'Someone I hired to drive me around.'

'Extraordinary looking chauffeur, isn't he?'

I smiled. 'His driving is pretty hair-raising as well.'

'Tell me about this man we're going to see.'

'I don't know much, really. He said his name was Johan Petersen . . .'

Arne grunted. 'There are dozens of Johan Petersens.'

'He said he was at the races the day Bob Sherman disappeared. He said he would like to tell me something about that. He said he lived at Lillehammer and worked there in the timber yard. I asked him to come to Oslo, but he said he couldn't take the day off. He said he'd meet me during his lunch break today. It was

225

very difficult to understand him clearly, as he spoke so little English. It'll be fine with you there.'

Arne nodded, blinking away as usual. The train took things easily, sliding quietly through the outer suburbs in a typically unhurried Norwegian fashion.

'How will you know him?'

'He said he would know me. All I have to do is walk down towards the bridge carrying an English news-paper.'

'Did you bring one?'

I nodded. 'In my coat pocket.'

The train was well heated. Coats were expected to be shed, and there was a rail at the rear equipped with hangers, where Arne's coat and mine hung side by side.

The line ran north through farmland and woods and alongside an extensive lake. On any other day I would have enjoyed the journey but it was extraordinary how a little fear could keep the mind focused close at hand. Old yellow eyes and his pal were a sight too near for comfort, and I'd developed an even worse over-the-shoulder compulsion through passengers walking up the centre aisle through the train. Every bang of the door from one carriage to the next had me looking to make sure.

A woman in a blue overall pushed a trolley into the carriage, selling from it hot drinks, biscuits and sweets. Arne bought me coffee. The trolley trundled away, and bang went the door behind her.

We stopped lengthily at a largish town, Hamar, a

junction with masses of open windswept platforms and no air of shunting or bustle. Then on again, moving faster, on towards Lillehammer. Two and a half hours, altogether, on the train.

'I missed you at the races on Sunday,' Arne said.

'Yes. I meant to go, but it was so cold.'

He gave me a look of friendly contempt.

'I might be going home soon,' I said.

'Are you?' He was surprised. 'I thought . . . you'd never leave us without finding out . . .'

'Well, after this trip today we should know a lot more. With a bit of luck. And then there's the key . . .'

'What key?'

'I found a luggage-locker key stuck in Bob Sherman's riding helmet.'

'You didn't!'

I nodded and told him about the trail to Paddy O'Flaherty's. 'So you see, although I'll go home soon, we should have most of the answers.'

Arne was enthusiastic. 'That's great,' he said. 'All we have to do now is find what's in the locker which the key fits.' A thought struck him. 'Perhaps it's that money. In the canvas bags . . . you know, the money that was stolen.'

'It's a thought,' I said. I didn't launch into explaining what actually had been in the locker; time enough for that later, as from the way the other passengers were standing up and putting on their coats it was clear we had nearly arrived. The train ran beside Lake Mjøsa and in the distance I could see the timber yard, with acres of pine tree logs floating in the water.

Arne held my coat for me, and I his for him. He smiled a little sadly.

'Kari and I will miss you.'

'I'll be back one day. I like Norway very much.'

He nodded. The train passed the end of the bridge to Gjøvik, climbed a hill slowly, inched into Lillehammer station, and sighed to a stop. We stepped out into a stinging wind under a grey cloud-filled sky. So much, I thought, for all those happy holiday posters of sun and snow and people on skis showing their suntans and teeth. It was odd, too, how none of the far frozen north railway stations had sheltering roofs over the platforms. Perhaps no one ever stood waiting in the open air, so that roofs were redundant and there was some point in them all still looking like the last scene in *Anna Karenina*.

'Are you coming, David?' Arne said.

'Yeah.' I stopped looking around vaguely and followed him through the main doors into the booking hall. At the far end of the platform two men, by-passing the station buildings, had set off quickly in the general direction of the road to the bridge. One was big. The other, of the same build as my attacker in the flat. They were too far away for me to swear to it in court.

But I was sure, just the same.

The small booking hall was scattered with prospective travellers wearing limbo expressions, waiting for time to pass. There were seats round the walls, doors to washrooms, a window for buying tickets: all the amenities in one central area. Arne said he wanted to make a telephone call before we set off to the meeting with our informer down the road.

'Carry on,' I said amiably.

I watched him through the glass wall of the booth feeding money into the slot and talking earnestly into the mouthpiece. He talked for a good long time, and came out smiling.

'All done. Let's go,' he said.

'Arne . . .' I hesitated. 'I know this is going to sound silly, but I don't want to go.'

He looked dumbstruck. 'But why not? This man might have seen who killed Bob Sherman.'

'I know. But . . . I can't explain it. I have . . . the weirdest feeling of premonition. I've had it before . . . I can't . . . I can't ignore it. Something tells me not to go. So I'm not going.'

'But David,' he said. 'That's crazy.'

'I can't help it. I'm not going.'

'But what about the man?'

I said helplessly, 'I don't know.'

Arne grew impatient. He tried insults. He tried persuasion. I wouldn't budge.

In the end he said, 'Give me the newspaper. I'll go and meet him myself.'

'But,' I objected, 'if my premonition means there is some danger down that road, it must be dangerous for you as well. I had a premonition about a street once before . . . I wouldn't go down it, and a few seconds later several tons of scaffolding collapsed on to where I would have been. Ever since then, when I've a strong feeling against doing something, I don't do it.'

He blinked at me earnestly. 'If I see any scaffolding, I'll keep away from it. But we must see this Johan Petersen and hear his story. Give me the newspaper.'

Reluctantly I handed him the previous day's *Express*. 'I'll wait for you here,' I said.

He nodded, still not pleased, and set off on his own. I chose a place to sit at one end of one of the bench seats, with solid wall at my back and on one side. On my other side sat a plump teenage girl in a shaggy sheepskin coat eating herring sandwiches noisily.

A few people came. A train arrived and took most of them away, including my neighbour. Time passed very slowly.

An hour and a half between our arrival and the train back to Oslo. An hour and a half to kill. Correction, I thought wryly. To stay alive. I wished I smoked or bit my nails or went in for yoga. I wished my heart wouldn't jump every time people walked past the window in pairs. I wished I knew what views yellow eyes and brown eyes held on murdering in public, because if only I was sure they wouldn't risk it I could save myself a lot of fretting. As it was I sat and waited and slowly sweated, hoping I'd judged their limit right.

When passengers for the Oslo train started arriving

and buying tickets I bought two myself for Arne and me. I asked particularly for the most public pair of seats in the carriage, as observed on the way up, and although I had difficulty explaining what I wanted as the ticket seller spoke little English, I got them.

Back in my careful corner I found myself flanked by an elderly man with an ear-flapped cap topping cream-coloured skin over an elongated skull. He had heard me speak English at the ticket window and was eager to tell me that he'd been in England the year before on holiday with his son and daughter-in-law. I encouraged him a bit, and got in return a minute by minute conducted tour from Tower Hill via Westminster Abbey to the National Gallery. By the time Arne came back, a quarter of an hour before train time, we were chatting away like old friends.

Arne was looking anxious. I stood up to meet him, gesturing to the elderly man and saying, 'We've been talking about London . . .'

Arne glanced at the man without really seeing him and abruptly interrupted. 'He didn't come.'

'Oh no,' I said.

Arne shook his head. 'I waited. I walked down to the bridge twice. I showed the newspaper. No one spoke to me. No one even walked past looking as if they were looking for anyone.'

I made frustrated noises. 'What a bloody nuisance. I'm so sorry, Arne, to have wasted a whole day for you . . . but he sounded so definite. Perhaps he was

231

delayed and couldn't help it. Perhaps we could telephone the timber yard . . .'

'I did,' he said. 'They haven't any Johan Petersen working there.'

We stared at each other.

I said depressedly, 'I banked so much on his giving us some really vital information.'

He looked at me uncertainly.

'My premonition was all wrong then,' I said.

'I told you.'

'Yes, you did.'

He began to fish out his wallet.

'I've got the tickets,' I said, producing them. 'Two seats together.'

'Oh . . . good.'

The train arrived, dark red and silver, and we climbed aboard. The seats were all I'd hoped, right down at one end, with their backs to the wardrobe end but facing every other seat in the coach. By a stroke of luck my elderly friend of the London holiday took his place on the aisle three seats down. He had a clear view of Arne and me, and waved and smiled. I told Arne how friendly he had been. Like all Norwegians, I said.

Arne jerked a look over his shoulder. Only a row of hangers with coats; but he didn't look happy.

Two bright-eyed young girls came and sat in the two seats directly facing us. I moved my feet out of the way of theirs, and smiled at them. They smiled back and said something in their own language.

'I'm English,' I said, and they repeated 'English' and nodded and smiled again. 'And this is my friend Arne Kristiansen.' They put the introduction down to the eccentricity of foreigners, saying hello to him with giggles. Arne said hello back, but he was old enough to be their father and not interested in their girlish chat.

The train started back towards Oslo. We talked for a while about the non-appearance of Johan Petersen and I said we would just have to hope that he would telephone again.

'You'll let me know if he does?'

'Of course,' I said.

The lady in blue overalls arrived, pushing her comforts trolley down the aisle. I said it was my turn to buy the coffee, and despite Arne's protestations I did so. I also offered drinks to the two girls who thought it a great lark and went pink. They asked Arne to see if it was all right for them to have orangeade, as they didn't like coffee. The lady in blue overalls patiently attended to all Arne's translations and finally with a smile gave him my change.

Arne began to wear the hunted look he often did in crowds.

'Let's go somewhere quieter,' he said.

'You go,' I said. 'But I rather like it here.'

He shook his head, but he stayed.

To his relief and my regret the two young girls got off at Hamar, giggling goodbye with backward glances. No one embarked to take their empty places, but after the train had started again my elderly friend got to his feet and came inquiringly towards us.

'May I sit here with you?' he said. 'It is so interesting to talk about England.'

Too much for Arne. He rose abruptly to his feet and dived through to the next carriage. The door banged behind him.

'Have I upset your friend?' asked the elderly man anxiously. 'I am sorry.'

'He has problems,' I said. 'But not of your making.'

Relieved, he launched into more reminiscences which bored me to death but quite likely kept me alive. He was still there, talking inexhaustibly, as we drew into Oslo. And on the platform, flanked by Odin, stood Erik anxiously looking out for me, just as promised.

There wasn't much time left. If they were going to make an attempt now they were going to have to do it in the open.

I stepped off the train and turned towards Erik. And there between us, looking sickeningly businesslike, stood the two men I least wanted to see.

CHAPTER FIFTEEN

Battle never commenced.

Erik saw them at the same moment I did, and yelled 'Police' at the top of his lungs.

Every person within earshot stopped to look.

'Police,' he yelled again, pointing at yellow eyes and brown eyes. 'These are thieves. Fetch the police.' And he repeated it in Norwegian, very loudly.

It broke their nerve. They looked round at the growing circle staring at them wide-eyed, and suddenly made a bolt for the exit. No one made much effort to stop them, and the chief expression on every beholder's face was astonishment.

Erik strode up to me and pumped my hand.

'Just putting your theory into practice,' he said.

I looked blank.

He explained. 'Knut told me you didn't think they'd kill you while people were looking. So I just got a few people to look.'

'Thanks.'

'Call it quits,' he said with a grin, and patted Odin.

I discovered that the palms of my hands were wet and a lot of me was quietly shaking.

'I need a telephone,' I said.

'You need a good stiff drink.'

'That too.'

I rang Knut. 'I'm back at the terminus,' I said.

'Thank God for that.'

'Did it work?'

I asked with some intensity, because I'd risked my skin for nearly seven shivery hours and no one could be entirely objective after that.

'Yes,' he said, but there was an odd note of reservation in his voice. 'At least . . . *Ja.*'

'What's the matter?'

'You had better come here, to the police station. It will be easier to explain.'

'All right.'

I stepped outside the box and almost fell over Odin who was lying across the door like a medieval page. He gave me a reproachful look, stood nonchalantly up, and yawned.

I asked Erik, 'Did you see Arne Kristiansen anywhere?'

'Who?'

I scanned the crowd without success. 'Never mind. I expect he's gone home.'

In gathering dusk Erik drove sedately (only one near-miss) to the police building, where I went upstairs and found Knut sitting alone and chewing a pencil. He gestured me to the visitors' chair and produced only the vestige of a smile.

'Well . . . we did everything you suggested,' he said. 'We planted the chart in a locker at Fornebu and put the key loose in the helmet in your room at the Grand. We sprinkled anthracene dust over every surface an intruder would touch and we waited at Fornebu to see if anyone would come.'

He rattled the pencil along his teeth.

'Someone did come,' he said.

'Who?'

He sighed. 'You'd better come and see.'

He led the way out of his meagre office and down an uncarpeted corridor, and stopped outside a cream painted door. Bright light from inside shone through a small glass panel let into the wood at viewing height.

'Look,' Knut said.

I looked.

The room was small and bare, containing only a simple table and three chairs. One chair was occupied by a young uniformed policeman looking stolid. On another, smoking quietly and as calm as if he were back in his own boardroom, sat Per Bjørn Sandvik.

I pulled my head away from the glass and stared at Knut.

'Come back to my office,' he said.

We went back and sat down as before.

'He came to Fornebu and opened the locker,' Knut said. 'That was at . . .' he consulted a note-pad, ' . . . fourteen thirty-five hours precisely. He removed the chart from the locker and put it in an inside pocket. I myself and two other officers went up to him as he was walking away from the lockers and asked him to accompany us to this police station. He seemed surprised but not . . . not deeply disturbed. I have arrested so many people . . . Per Bjørn Sandvik did not behave like a guilty man.'

He rubbed thumb and finger down his nose.

'I don't know what to make of him, David. He shrugged and said he would come with us if we liked, but he said almost nothing else until we got back here. He was completely calm. No sign of stress. None at all. He has been here now for about an hour and a half, and he has been calm and courteous the whole time.'

'What explanation did he give?'

'We went into that interview room and sat on the chairs, with a constable to take notes. Mr Sandvik offered me a cigarette. He said he had only been trying to help the investigation into Bob Sherman's death. He said Arne Kristiansen had telephoned to say that you had found a key which might lead to useful information, so he went to the Grand Hotel to fetch the key, which he recognized as having come from Fornebu, as he has often used those lockers in the past. So he went to the airport . . . to see what Bob Sherman had left there. He said he thought it might have been the missing money, but it was only a paper. He hadn't done more than glance at it when we stopped him.'

'Did he give any reason for doing all this himself and not waiting for Arne or me to get back or enlisting the help of the police?'

'*Ja.*' He smiled a small tight smile to mock me. 'He said Arne asked him to do it. Arne wanted to prove to the racecourse committee that he was worth his salary as an investigator, so he telephoned to Sandvik as a member of the racecourse committee to tell him about the key. Arne apparently said that if he and Mr Sandvik helped with the case, the committee would not be able to give all the praise to you.'

'What do you think?'

He looked depressed. 'Per Bjørn Sandvik is a leader of industry. He is much respected. He is being very reasonable, but if we keep him here much longer he will be angry.'

'And your superiors will lean on you?'

'Er . . . *ja.*'

I thought.

'Don't worry, Knut,' I said. 'We've got the right man.'

'But he is so confident.'

I nodded. 'He's working on a false assumption.'

'What's that?'

'He thinks I'm dead.'

*

Per Bjørn Sandvik got a very nasty shock indeed when I walked into the interview room.

Muscles round his eyes and mouth contracted sharply, and his pale skin went perceptibly paler. But his resilience was extraordinary. Within three seconds he was smiling pleasantly with the deceptive lack of agitation which was so confusing Knut.

'David!' he said as if in welcome, yet I could almost hear and certainly sense the alarm bells going at panic strength.

'I'm afraid this isn't the happiest of meetings,' I said.

He was making such an urgent reappraisal that the muscles round his eyes were moving in tiny rhythmical spasms: which booted out of me any hint of complacency, because people who could think as quickly and intently as that in such adverse circumstances had brains to beware of.

Knut followed me into the room and told the young policeman to fetch another chair. While he went to get it I watched Per Bjørn finish reorganizing his thoughts. Infinitesimally, he relaxed. Too soon, I reckoned; and I couldn't afford to be wrong.

The extra chair came, and we all sat down round the bare table as if to a simple business discussion.

I said, 'It must have occurred to you by now that there was no Johan Petersen at Lillehammer.'

'I don't understand,' he said pleasantly in his high, distinct diction. 'I thought we were talking about the locker key and Fornebu airport.'

'We're talking about Arne Kristiansen,' I said.

A pause. I waited. But he was too cautious now to take any step without prospecting for quicksand, and after some time, when he said nothing, I invited him a little further along the path.

'You shouldn't rely on Arne,' I said. 'Arne is deep in, up to the neck.'

No response.

'Come to think of it,' I said. 'Up to his neck and over his head, considering the amount of swimming he's done.'

No reaction.

'All that messing around in the fjord,' I said. 'There was me thinking Arne had drowned, while all the time he had a scuba suit on under his red anorak. Nice snug black rubber with yellow seams, fitting right up over his head to keep him warm.' I'd seen the black-and-yellow under his anorak. It had taken me days to realize it had been rubber. But then that chug down the fjord happened before I'd begun to be sure that Arne was on the other side.

'A strong swimmer, Arne,' I said. 'A tough all-round sportsman. So there he is standing up in the dinghy waving his arms about as if to warn the speedboat not to run us down while all the time signalling to it that yes, this was the dinghy it was supposed to be sinking. This dinghy, not some other poor innocent slob out on a fishing trip. Arne swam ashore, reported an accident, reported me drowned.'

A pause.

'I don't know what you're talking about,' Per Bjørn said, and patiently sighed.

'I'm talking about Arne putting on his scuba suit and diving into the pond at Øvrevoll to get Bob Sherman out of it.'

Silence.

Arne had been sick when he saw the month-dead body. At night, when he'd fished Bob out and wrapped him in tarpaulin it couldn't have seemed so bad: but in the light of a drizzly day it had hit him a bull's-eye in the stomach.

'I'm talking about Arne being the one person who could be sure no one saw him putting bodies into ponds, taking them out again, and later putting them back again. Arne was security officer. He could come and go on that racecourse as he pleased. No one would think it odd if he were on the racecourse first, last, and during the night. But he could also make sure that the night watchman saw nothing he shouldn't, because the night watchman would carry out any attention-distracting task Arne gave him.'

Nothing.

'This is speculation,' he said.

Knut sat still and quiet, keeping his promise that he would make no comment, whatever I said. The young policeman's pencil had made scarcely a mark on the page.

'Arne stole the money himself,' I said. 'To provide a reason for Bob Sherman's disappearance.'

'Nonsense.'

'The impression of most people in the officials' room was that the money had been put in the safe. And so it had. Arne himself had put it there, as he usually does. He has keys to every gate, every building, every door on the place. He didn't take the money during the five minutes that the room happened to be empty. He had all night to do it in.'

'I don't believe it. Arne Kristiansen is a respected servant of the racecourse.'

He sat there listening to me with long-suffering courtesy as if I were a rather boring guest he was stuck with.

'Bob Sherman brought a packet of papers with him from England,' I said.

'Yes, you've already asked about that. I told you I couldn't help you.'

'Unfortunately for him, he was curious. He opened the package and saw what he had no business to see. He must have done this on the flight over, as he left some of the contents in a locker at Fornebu.'

Per Bjørn slowly turned his good-looking head until he was facing Knut, not me, and he spoke to him in Norwegian. Knut made gestures of regret and helplessness, and said nothing at all.

'Bob Sherman was too fond of schemes for getting rich quickly,' I said. 'He was being paid for bringing the envelope, but it seemed to him that he could push the price up a bit. Very much his mistake, of course. He got bonked on the head for his pains. And no one discovered until long after he was dead and in the pond that when he'd opened the envelope he'd taken something out.'

Per Bjørn sat impassively, waiting for the annoying gnat to stop buzzing around him.

I buzzed a bit more.

'Because what he took out was in a way a duplication of what he left in.'

That one hit home. His eye muscles jumped. He knew that I'd noticed. He smiled.

I said, 'Bob Sherman took the precaution of hiding the key to the Fornebu locker in his racing helmet. By the time he was brought out of the pond it had been discovered that he had removed a paper from the envelope, but a search of his waterlogged clothes and overnight bag failed to produce any sign of it. So did a search of his house in England. By the time I realized what must be going on, and came to wonder if Bob had somehow hidden the missing object in his racing saddle or helmet, others had had the same idea. His saddle, which had stayed on its peg in the changing room for a month after he disappeared, was suddenly nowhere to be found.'

He sat. Quiet.

'However, the helmet with the saddle was no longer

Bob's but Paddy O'Flaherty's. I told Arne about the exchange. I told him I'd found the key.'

Per Bjørn crossed one leg over the other and took out his cigarettes. He offered them round, then when no one accepted, returned his case to his pocket and lit his own with a practised flick on a gas lighter. The hand which held the lighter was rock steady.

'I didn't tell him that we had already opened the locker and seen what it contained,' I said. 'We wanted to find out who else besides Arne was looking for the missing paper, so we gave that person an opportunity of finding it.'

'Ingenious,' he said. 'What a pity you had made the fundamental mistake of believing Arne Kristiansen to be connected with Bob Sherman's death. If he had been guilty of all you say, of course it would have been an excellent trap. As it is, of course . . .'

He delicately shrugged. Knut looked worried.

'There was the problem of the two men who searched Bob Sherman's house,' I said. 'If we didn't decoy them away they would be available to fetch the key and open the locker. So we provided an urgent reason for them to leave Oslo. We invented, in fact, a possible eye-witness to the killing of Bob Sherman. I told only Arne Kristiansen that I was going to Lille-hammer to meet this man, and I asked Arne to come with me. On the train I told him about the key and said that as soon as I got back I was going to give it to the police. I told him that the police were expecting me to report to them at once on my return, to tell them what the man in Lillehammer had said. This meant to Arne that if I didn't return the hunt would be on immediately and there might be no later opportunity to get into my room for the key. It had to be done quickly. A risk had to be taken.'

I paused.

'You took it,' I said.

'No.'

'You believed no one knew of the existence of the key except Arne and myself. You were wrong. You believed there was a possible eye-witness to Bob's murder and you sent your two assassins to deal with him. You expected them also to kill me as well. They aren't very successful at that. You should sack them.'

'This is ridiculous,' he said.

I said, 'I asked the reception desk at the Grand not to worry if anyone asked for my room number or my door key.' And extremely odd they'd thought it, after all the hide and seek of the previous days. 'We made it as easy as we could.'

He said nothing.

Knut had sprinkled the room with anthracene dust, which clung invisibly to any clothes or flesh which touched it and showed up with fluorescence under a strong ultra-violet light. Anyone denying he'd been in my room would have been proved to be lying. But Per Bjørn had out-thought that one and hadn't denied it. He must have done a great deal of fast figuring during his non-speaking ride from Fornebu to the police station. He couldn't have known about the anthracene, but he must have guessed that a trap so complicated in some respects wasn't likely to be naïve in others.

I said, 'The paper you were looking for is a chart of a core taken from area twenty-five/six of the North Sea.'

He absorbed that shock as if he were made throughout of expanded polystyrene.

I gave him some more. 'It was stolen from the Wessex-Wells Research Laboratory in Dorset, England, and the information it contains was the property of the Interpetro Oil Company. It is a chart showing exceptionally rich oil-bearing rock of high porosity and good permeability at a depth of thirteen thousand feet.'

It seemed to me that he had almost stopped breathing. He sat totally without movement, smoke from the cigarette between his fingers rising in a column as straight as honesty.

I said, 'The Interpetro Oil Company isn't part of the consortium to which your own company belongs, but it is or was mainly Norwegian owned, and the well in question is in the Norwegian area of the North Sea. Immediately after Bob Sherman brought his package to Norway, the Interpetro shares started an upward movement on the world stock markets. Although a great deal of secrecy surrounds the buying, I'm told that the most active purchasers were in the Middle

East. You would know far better than I do whether it is to Norway's advantage to have one of her most promising oil fields largely bought up by oil-producing rivals.'

Not a flicker.

I said, 'Norway has never really forgiven the citizens who collaborated with the Nazis. How would they regard one of their most respected businessmen who sold advance news of their best oil field to the Middle East for his own personal gain?'

He uncrossed his legs and recrossed them the other way. He tapped the ash off his cigarette on to the floor, and inhaled a deep lungful of smoke.

'I wish,' he said, 'to telephone to my lawyer. And to my wife.'

CHAPTER SIXTEEN

Knut and I went back to his office and sat one each side of his desk.

'Can you prove it?' he said.

'We can prove he went to the Grand, fetched the key and opened the locker.'

'Anything else?'

I said gloomily, 'It's circumstantial. A good defence lawyer could turn everything inside out.'

Knut chewed his pencil.

'The scandal will ruin him,' he said.

I nodded. 'I'll bet he's got a fortune tucked away somewhere safe, though.'

'But,' Knut said, 'he must care more for his reputation than for just money, otherwise he would simply have left the country instead of having Bob Sherman killed.'

'Yes.'

We sat in silence.

'You are tired,' Knut said.

'Yeah. So are you.'

He grinned and looked suddenly very like Erik.

I said, 'Your brother told me Per Bjørn Sandvik was in the Resistance during the war.'

'*Ja*. He was.'

'Nothing wrong with his nerve,' I said. 'Nothing then, nothing now.'

'And we are not the Gestapo,' Knut said. 'He knows we will not torture him. We must seem feeble to him, after what he risked when he was young. He is not going to give in and confess. Not ever.'

I agreed.

'These two men,' I said. 'Yellow eyes and brown eyes. They're too young to have been in the Resistance themselves. But . . . is there a chance their fathers were? Arne's father was. Could you run a check on the group Per Bjørn belonged to, and see if any of them fathered yellow eyes?'

'You ask such impossible things.'

'And it's a very long shot indeed,' I sighed.

'I'll start tomorrow,' he said.

Some coffee arrived, very milky. I could have done with a treble scotch and a batch of Emma's scones.

'You know,' I said after another silence, 'there's something else. Some other way . . . There has to be.'

'What do you mean?'

'I mean . . . It was just luck finding that key. If Paddy hadn't swapped the helmets we would never have found the paper at Fornebu.' I drank the coffee. It wasn't strong enough to deal with anything but thirst.

'But . . . they tried to kill me before they knew the chart wasn't in the pond with Bob Sherman. So there must be something else which they couldn't afford for me to find.'

I put down the cup with a grimace.

'But what?' Knut asked.

'God knows.'

'Something I missed,' he said with gloom.

'Why would they think I would see it if you didn't?'

'Because you do,' he said. 'And Arne knows it.'

Arne . . . My friend Arne.

'Why didn't he kill you himself, out on the fjord?' Knut asked. 'Why didn't he just bang you on the head and push you overboard?'

'It isn't that easy to bang someone on the head when you're sitting at opposite ends of a small dinghy. And besides . . . leading a beast to the abattoir and slitting its neck are two different things.'

'I don't understand.'

'Arne was keen for me to die but wouldn't do it himself.'

'How do you know?'

'Because he didn't. Over the last few weeks he's had more chance than anybody, but he didn't do it.'

'You couldn't be sure he wouldn't.'

'He's a complex person but his attitudes are all fixed . . . if he didn't do it the first time he wouldn't do it afterwards.'

A few more minutes dawdled by while I tried to concentrate on what I hadn't discovered.

Useless, I thought.

Yesterday, I thought, I didn't know who had manipulated Interpetro Oil. Today I did. Did that make any difference?

'Oh my Christ,' I said, and nearly fell out of my chair.

'What is it?' Knut said.

'I'm bloody mad.'

'What do you mean?'

'You remember that bomb . . .'

'Well, of course I do.'

'It was such a sloppy way to kill someone,' I said. 'It might have gone off before we got back to the car . . . It didn't kill us, so we thought of it as a failure. But it didn't fail. Not a bit. It was a roaring success. It did just what it was meant to.'

'David . . .'

'Do you remember where I was going that afternoon? I didn't go, because the bomb stopped me. I'm so damned stupid . . . it isn't *what* I haven't seen, it's *who*.'

He just stared.

'*It's Mikkel Sandvik.*'

I telephoned to the College of Gol and spoke to the headmaster.

'Oh, but Mikkel isn't here,' he said. 'His father tele-phoned on Sunday morning to say that Mikkel must go and visit his aunt, who was dying and asking for him.'

'Where does the aunt live?'

'I don't know. Mr Sandvik talked to Mikkel himself.'

There was some speaking in the background, and then he said, 'My wife says Mikkel told her his Aunt Berit was dying. He went to catch the Bergen train. We don't know where he went after that . . . Why don't you ask his father?'

'Good idea,' I said.

'What now?' Knut said, when I told him.

'I think . . . I'll go and see Mrs Sandvik, and see if she'll tell me where Mikkel is.'

'All right. And I will do what I must about keeping Mr Sandvik here all night.' He sighed. 'A man like that . . . it doesn't seem right to put him in a cell.'

'Don't let him go,' I said.

'Oh no.'

Erik had gone home long ago but Knut reckoned I was on police business and sent me to the Sandvik house in a police car. I walked through the arch into the courtyard, turned right, and rang the bell outside the well-lit imposing front door.

A heavy middle-aged woman opened it. She wore frumpy clothes and no make-up, and had a positive, slightly forbidding manner.

'*Ja?*' she said inquiringly.

253

I explained who I was and asked to see Mrs Sandvik.

'I am Mrs Sandvik. I spoke to you on the telephone a few days ago.'

'That's right.' I swallowed my surprise. I had thought she would already have known about her husband being at the police station, but apparently he hadn't yet made his two calls. When we had left him, Knut had said he would arrange for a telephone to be taken to the interview room and plugged into the socket there, which I supposed took time. No one was positively rushing to provide facilities for a suspect, not even for Per Bjørn Sandvik.

It made it easier, however, for me to ask questions.

'Come inside,' she said. 'It is cold with the door open.'

I stepped into the hall. She invited me no farther.

'Mikkel?' she said in surprise. 'He is at school. I told you.'

I explained about his Aunt Berit.

'He has no Aunt Berit.'

Wow.

'Er . . .' I said. 'Does he know anyone at all called Berit?'

She raised her eyebrows. 'Is this important?'

'I cannot go home until I have seen Mikkel. I am sorry.'

She shrugged. After a longish pause for thought she said, 'Berit is the name of an old nurse of my husband.

254

I do not know if Mikkel knows any other person called Berit. I expect so.'

'Where does your husband's old nurse live?'

'I don't know.'

She couldn't remember the old nurse's surname, and she wasn't sure if she was still alive. She said her husband would be able to tell me, when he came home. She opened the door with finality for me to leave, and with a distinct feeling of cowardice, I left. Per Bjørn had smashed up her secure world and he would have to tell her about it himself.

'He might be with his father's old nurse,' I told Knut. 'And he might not.'

He reflected. 'If he caught the Bergen train, perhaps the Gol ticket office would remember him.'

'Worth a try. But he could be anywhere by now. Anywhere in the world.'

'He's barely seventeen,' Knut said.

'That's old, these days.'

'How did Mrs Sandvik take the news of her husband's arrest?'

'I didn't tell her. I thought Per Bjørn should do that.'

'But he has!'

'She didn't know,' I said blankly.

'But,' Knut said, 'I am sure he made his two calls almost half an hour ago.'

'Bloody hell,' I said.

He steamed out of the office at twenty knots and yelled at several unfortunate subordinates. When he returned he was carrying a piece of paper and looking grim, worried and apologetic all at once.

'They find it difficult not to obey a man with such prestige,' he said. 'He told them to wait outside the door while he spoke to his wife and his lawyer, as both calls were of a private nature. They did what he said.' He looked at the paper in his hand. 'At least they had the sense to dial the numbers for him, and to write them down. They are both Oslo numbers.'

He handed the paper over for me to see. One of the numbers meant nothing. The other meant too much.

'He talked to Arne,' I said.

I pressed the bell outside Arne's flat and after a long interval Kari opened the door.

'David.' She seemed neither surprised nor pleased to see me. She seemed drained.

'Come in,' she said.

The flat seemed somehow colder, less colourful, much quieter than before.

'Where's Arne?' I said.

'He's gone.'

'Where to?'

'I don't know.'

'Tell me everything he did since he came home.'

She gave me an empty stare, then turned away and

walked through to the sitting-room. I followed her. She sat on the cream-coloured sofa and shivered. The stove no longer glowed with warmth and welcome and the stereo record player was switched off.

'He came home upset. Well . . . he's been upset ever since this Bob Sherman thing started. But today he was very worried and puzzled and disturbed. He played two long records and marched about . . . he couldn't keep still.'

Her voice had the calmness of shock. The reality of whatever had happened had not yet tipped her into anger or fear or despair: but tomorrow, I thought, she might suffer all three.

'He rang Per Bjørn Sandvik's house twice, but they said he wasn't in. It seemed to worry him very much.'

There was a tray on the coffee table in front of her laden with an untouched dish of open sandwiches. They made me feel frantically hungry as I hadn't eaten since a pin-sized breakfast, but she gave them an indifferent glance and said, 'He left them. He said he couldn't . . .'

Try me, I thought: but hostessing was far out of her mind.

'Then Per Bjørn Sandvik rang here. Only a little while ago . . . but it seems hours and hours . . . Arne was relieved at first, but then . . . he went so quiet . . . I knew something was wrong.'

'What did he say to Per Bjørn? Can you remember?'

'He said *Ja*, and No. He listened a long time. He said . . . I think he said . . . don't worry, I'll find him.'

257

'That was all?'

She nodded. 'Then he went into the bedroom and he was so quiet . . . I went to see what was the matter. He was sitting on the bed, looking at the floor. He looked up at me when I came. His eyes were . . . I don't know . . . dead.'

'And then?'

'He got up and began packing a suitcase. I asked him . . . he said don't worry me . . . so I just stood there. He packed . . . he threw things into the case . . . and he was muttering away, mostly about you.'

She looked at me intently but still with the numb lack of emotion.

'He said . . . "I told him, I told him David would beat him . . . I told him at the beginning . . . he still says David hasn't beaten him but he has, he has . . ." I asked Arne what he was talking about but I don't think he even heard me.' She pressed her fingers against her forehead, rubbing the smooth skin. 'Arne said . . . "David . . . David knew all day . . . he made the trap and put himself into it as bait . . . he knew all day." Then he said something about you using some girls and an old man, and something about orangeade . . . and a premonition you invented. He said he knew you would be the end of everything; he said so before you came.'

She looked at me with the sudden awakening of awareness and the beginnings of hostility.

'What did you do?' she asked.

'I'm sorry, Kari. I gave Arne and Per Bjørn Sandvik

a chance to show they knew more than they ought about Bob Sherman's death, and they took it.'

'More than they ought ...?' she repeated vaguely: then overwhelmingly understood. 'Oh no. Oh no. Not Arne.' She stood up abruptly. 'I don't believe it.' But she already did.

'I still don't know who killed Bob Sherman,' I said. 'I think Arne does know. I want to talk to him.'

'He's not coming back. He said ... he would write, and send for me. In a few weeks.' She looked forlorn. 'He took the car.' She paused. 'He kissed me.'

'I wish ...' I said uselessly, and she caught the meaning in my voice though the words weren't spoken.

'Yes,' she said. 'In spite of everything ... he likes you too.'

It was still not yet eight o'clock and Per Bjørn was still in the interview room when I got back to the police station.

'His lawyer is with him,' Knut said morosely. 'We won't get a word out of him now.'

'We haven't had so many already.'

'No.' He flicked the paper with the telephone numbers which was lying on his desk. 'This other number ... it isn't the lawyer's.'

'Whose, then?'

'It's a big second-class hotel near the docks. Dozens of incoming calls; they couldn't remember one more than any other. I have sent a policeman down there with a description of the man with yellow eyes.'

'Mm. Whoever he spoke to at the hotel then telephoned the lawyer.'

'*Ja*,' he said. 'It must be so. Unless Arne did.'

'I don't think so, from what his wife said.'

'He had gone?'

I nodded. 'In his car.'

He put his hand again on the telephone. 'We will find the number and put out an alert: and also check with the airport and the frontier posts with Sweden.'

'I know the number.' I told it to him. He looked surprised, but I said, 'I've been in his car . . . and I've a memory for numbers. Don't know why.'

He put out his alerts and sat tapping his pencil against his teeth.

'And now we wait,' he said.

We waited precisely five seconds before the first call came through. He scooped up the receiver with a speed which betrayed his inner pressure, and listened intently.

'*Ja*,' he said eventually. '*Ja . . . takk*. Thank you.'

He put down the receiver and relayed the news.

'That was the policeman I sent to the hotel. He says the man with yellow eyes has been staying there for a week, but this evening he paid his bill and left. He gave no address. He was known to the hotel as L. Horgen. My policeman says that unfortunately the room has already been cleaned because the hotel is busy, but he has directed them to leave it empty until we've searched it and tried for fingerprints. Excuse me while I send a team to do that.'

He went out of the office and was gone a fair time, but when he came back he had more to tell.

'We've found Arne's car. It is parked not far from the quay of the Nansen shipping line, and one of their ships left for Copenhagen an hour ago. We are radioing to the ship and to Copenhagen to pick him up.'

'Don't let them relax at Fornebu,' I said.

He looked at me.

I grinned faintly. 'Well . . . If I wanted to slip out by air I'd leave my car beside a shipping line and take a taxi to the airport. And Arne and I once discussed quite a lot of things like that.'

'He'd know you'd guess, then.'

'I'd pin more hope on the ship if he'd left his car at the airport.'

He shook his head and sighed. 'A good thing you're not a crook,' he said.

A young policeman knocked, came in, and spoke to Knut.

He translated for me. 'Mr Sandvik's lawyer wants to see me, with his client. I'll go along to the interview room . . . Do you want to come?'

'Please,' I said.

With Per Bjørn, his lawyer, Knut, me, and a note-taking policeman all inside with the door shut, the small interview room looked overcrowded with dark suits and solemnity. The other four sat on the hard chairs round the plain table and I stood leaning against the door, listening to a long conversation of which I understood not a word.

Per Bjørn pushed back his chair, crossed his legs and set fire to a cigarette, much as before. His lawyer, a heavy self-possessed man of obvious worldly power, was speaking in an authoritative voice and making Knut perceptibly more nervous minute by minute. But Knut survived uncracked and although when he answered he sounded friendly and apologetic, the message he got across was 'No.'

It angered the lawyer more than the client. He stood up, towering over Knut, and delivered a severe caution. Knut looked worried, stood up in his turn, and shook his head. After that the young policeman was sent on an errand, presently returning with a sergeant and an escort.

Knut said, 'Mr Sandvik . . .', and waited.

Per Bjørn stood up slowly and stubbed out his filter tip. He looked impassively at the escort and walked calmly towards them. When he drew level with me at the doorway he stopped, turned his head, and stared very deliberately at my face.

But whatever he was thinking, nothing at all showed in his eyes, and he spoke not a word.

Knut went home, but I spent the night in his office sleeping on the floor on blankets and pillows borrowed from the cells; and I daresay I was less comfortable than the official guest downstairs.

'What's wrong with the Grand?' Knut said, when I asked him to let me stay.

'Yellow eyes is on the loose,' I said. 'And who knows what instructions Per Bjørn gave him?'

Knut looked at me thoughtfully. 'You think there's more to come?'

'Per Bjørn is still fighting.'

'*Ja*,' he sighed. 'I think so too.'

He sent a policeman out to bring me a hot meal from a nearby restaurant, and in the morning at eight o'clock he came back with a razor. He himself, trim in his uniform, seemed to have shed yesterday like a skin and arrived bright eyed and awake to the new day. I shivered blearily in my crumpled clothes and felt like a reject from a doss house.

At eight forty-five the telephone rang. Knut picked up the receiver, listened, and seemed pleased with what he heard.

'*Ja. Ja. Takk*,' he said.

'What is it?'

He put the receiver back. 'We've had a message from Gol. The man who was on duty in the ticket office on Sunday remembers that a boy from the College bought a ticket to Finse.'

'Finse . . .' I thought back to my time-tables. 'On the Bergen line?'

'*Ja*. Finse is the highest town on the line. Up in the

mountains. I will find out if he is remembered at the station there. I will find out if anyone has seen him in the streets or knows if he is staying.'

'How long will that take?'

'One can't tell.'

'No.' I thought it over. 'Look . . . the train for Bergen leaves at ten, if I remember right. I'll catch it. Then if you hear that Mikkel is or isn't at Finse, perhaps you could get a message to me at one of the stops up the line.'

'Have you forgotten yellow eyes?'

'Unfortunately not,' I said.

He smiled. 'All right. I will send you to the station in a police car. Do you want a policeman to go with you?'

I thought. 'I might get further with Mikkel if I go alone.'

On the train I sat next to a total stranger, a cheerful young man with little English, and spent an uneventful journey looking out at peaceful fields and bright little dolls' houses scattered haphazardly on hillsides.

At Gol there was a written message.

'Young man disembarkation to Finse the Sunday. One knows not until where he gone. The questions is continue.'

'Thank you very much,' I said.

The train climbed slowly above the tree line into a landscape of blue-grey rock and green-grey water. Snow scattered the ground, at first in patches, then in

rofusion, and finally as a thin white rug over every
loping surface, with sharp rock edges like hatchets
howing through.

'Is small snow,' said my companion. 'In winter in
Finse is two metres.'

'Two metres deep?' I asked.

He nodded. '*Ja*. Is good for ski.'

The railway ran for a time alongside a fiercely cold-
looking wind-ruffled grey-green lake and slowed with
a sigh of relief into Finse.

'Is hot summer,' my friend said, looking around in
surprise. 'Is snow gone.'

He might think so, but I didn't. Snow still covered
everything worth mentioning, hot summer gone by or
not; and icicles dangled from every roof like stiff, glit-
tering fringes. Once out of the warmth of the train the
cold bit sharply and even in my ear-covering cap and
padded jacket I wrapped my arms round my chest in a
futile attempt to hold on to my body heat.

I was met by the bulk of the Finse police force in
the shape of a broadly smiling officer of turnstile-
blocking size.

'Mr Cleveland.' He shook my hand. 'We do not
know where is this boy Mikkel Sandvik. We have
not seen him in the village. There are not many
strangers here now. In the summer, and in the winter,
we have very many strangers. We have the big hotel,
for the ski. But now, not many. We have look for an
old woman who is called Berit. There are two. It is not

one, because she is in bed in the house of her son and she is ... er ... she is ... old.'

'Senile?' I suggested.

He didn't know the word. 'Very old,' he repeated.

'And the other Berit?'

'She lives in a house beside the lake. One and a half kilometres out of Finse. She goes away in the winter. Soon, now. She is a strong old woman. In the summer she takes people who come to fish, but they have all gone now. Usually on Wednesdays she comes for food, so we have not gone to see her. But she is late today. She comes in the mornings.'

'I'll go there,' I said, and listened to directions.

The way to the house of Berit-by-the-lake turned out to be merely a path which ran between the railway line and the shore, more a matter of small stones and pebbles through an area of boulders than any recognizable beaten track. With its roughnesses still half-covered with crusty ice, it was easy to imagine that once the new snows fell it would be entirely obliterated.

CHAPTER SEVENTEEN

I looked back.

A bend had taken Finse out of sight.

I looked forward. Nothing but the sketchy path picking its uncertain way through the snow-strewn boulders. Only on my right could be seen any evidence of humanity, and that was the railway. And then that too ran straight ahead behind a hill while the shore curved to the left, so that in the end there was just me and the stark unforgiving landscape, just me trudging through an energetic wind on a cold, wild and lonely afternoon.

The path snaked its way round two small bays and two small headlands, with the hillside on my right rising ever more steeply the farther I went, and then all of a sudden the house lay before me, standing alone on a flat stony area spread out like an apron into the lake.

The house was red. A strong crimson. Roof, walls, door, the lot. The colour stood out sharply against the grey and white of the shore and the darker grey-green of the water; and rising beyond it at the head of the lake stood dark towering cliffs, thrown up like a sudden mountain against the northern sky.

Maybe it was a grand, extraordinary, awe-inspiring sight. Maybe it should have swelled my spirit, uplifted my soul. Actually it inspired in me nothing more noble than a strong desire to retreat.

I stopped.

Surely Sandvik wouldn't have sent his son to this threatening place, even if he did urgently want to hide him. Surely Mikkel was half the world away by now, with Arne cantering post haste in his wake to look after him.

Damned bloody silly place to build a house, I thought. Enough to give anyone the creeps, living with a mountain on the doorstep.

I went on. The house had a landing stage with a motor boat tied to a post like a hitched horse in a Western. It also had looped up lace curtains and geraniums on the window sills. Red geraniums. Naturally.

I looked in vain for smoke from the chimney, and no one stared out at me as I approached.

I banged the knocker. The door was opened straight away by a ramrod-backed old woman, five feet tall, sharp eyed, entirely self possessed. Far, very far, from dying.

'*Ja?*' she said enquiringly.

'I'd like to talk to Mikkel,' I said.

She took a very brief pause to change languages,

nd then in a pure near-Scots accent said, 'Who are
ou?'

'I am looking for Mikkel.'

'Everyone is looking for Mikkel.' She inspected me
rom head to foot. 'Come in. It is cold.'

She showed me into the living-room, where everything was in process of being packed away in crates.
She gestured round with a fine-boned hand. 'I am
leaving now for the winter. It is beautiful here in the
summer, but not in winter.'

'I have a message from his father,' I said.

'Another one?'

'What do you mean?'

'Already one man came this morning. Then another.
Both of them said they had a message from his father.
And now you.' She looked at me straightly. 'That is
very many messages.'

'Yes . . . I have to find him.'

She put her head on one side. 'I told the others. I
cannot judge which of you I should not tell. So I will
tell you. He is on the mountain.'

I looked through the window to the wall of rock and
the end of the lake.

'Up there?'

'*Ja*. There is a cabin up there. I rent it to visitors in
the summer, but in the winter the snow covers it.
Mikkel went up there this morning to bring down the
things I do not want to leave there. He is a kind boy.'

'Who were the other men who came?'

269

'I don't know. The first one said his name was Kristiansen. They both said they would go up and help
Mikkel bring down the things, although I said it was
not necessary, there are not many things and he took
the sleigh.'

'The sleigh?'

'*Ja*. Very light. You can pull it.'

'Perhaps I had better go up there as well.'

'You have bad shoes.'

I looked down. City casuals, not built for snowy
mountains, and already darkly wet round the edges.

'Can't be helped,' I said.

She shrugged. 'I will show you the path. It is better
than the one round the lake.' She smiled faintly. 'I do
not walk to Finse. I go in the boat.'

'The second man,' I said. 'Did he have extraordinary
yellow eyes?'

'No.' She shook her head decisively. 'He was
ordinary. Very polite. Like you.' She smiled and pointed
through the window. 'The path starts over there behind
that big rock. It is not steep. It winds away from the
lake and then comes back. You will see it easily.'

I thanked her and set off, and found almost at once
that she was right about the shoes. One might be able
to see the path easily, but that was because it was a
well-worn track through the snow, patterned widely on
either side by the marks of skis, like a sort of mini
highway.

I slithered along in the brisk wind, working round

the hillside in a wide, ever upward-sloping U. But it proved to be not as far as I'd feared, because, long before I expected it, I came to the top of a small rise and found below me, suddenly only a few yards away, a sturdy little log hut, built to the traditional Norwegian pattern like a roofed box standing on a slightly smaller plinth.

It was already too late to make a careful inconspicuous approach. I stood there in full view of a small window: so I simply walked straight up and looked through it.

The cabin was dark inside and at first I thought it was empty. Then I saw him. Huddled in a corner, with his head bent over his knees, slowly rocking as if in pain.

There was only one small room. Only one door. I put my hand on its latch and opened it.

The movement galvanized the figure inside into action, and it was only something half seen, half instinctive, which had me leaping sideways away from the entrance with adrenalin scorching down to my toes. Blast from a shotgun roared through the doorway, and I pressed myself against the heavy log wall alongside and hoped to God it was impervious to pellets.

A voice shouted something hysterically from inside.

Not Arne's voice. Young. Stretched to breaking.

'Mikkel,' I said. 'I will not harm you. I am David Cleveland.'

Silence.

'Mikkel . . .'

'If you come in, I will shoot you.' His voice was naturally high pitched like his father's, and the tension in it had strung it up another octave.

'I only want to talk to you.'

'No. No. No.'

'Mikkel . . . You can't stay here for ever.'

'If you come in, I'll shoot.'

'All right . . . I'll talk from here.' I shivered with cold and wholeheartedly cursed him.

'I will not talk to you. Go away. Go away.'

I didn't answer. Five minutes passed with no sound except the blustering wind. Then his voice from inside, tight and frightened. 'Are you still there?'

'Yes,' I said.

'Go away.'

'We have to talk sometime. Might as well be now.'

'No.'

'Where is Arne Kristiansen?' I asked.

His reply was a high keening wail which raised goose-bumps up my spine. What followed it was a thoroughly normal sob.

I crouched down low and risked a quick look through the door. The gun lay in one hand on the floor and with the other he was trying to wipe away tears. He looked up and saw me, and again immediately began to aim.

I retreated smartly and stood up outside against the wall, as before.

'Why don't you tell me?' I said.

A long pause of several minutes.

'You can come in.'

I took another quick look. He was sitting straight legged on the floor with the gun pointing at the door.

'Come in,' he said. 'I won't shoot.'

'Put the gun on the floor and slide it away.'

'No.'

More time passed.

'The only way I'll talk,' he said, 'is if you come in. But I will keep the gun.'

I swallowed. 'All right.'

I stepped into the doorway. Looked down the double barrels. He sat with his back against the wall, holding the gun steady. A box of cartridges lay open beside him, with one or two scattered around.

'Shut the door,' he said. 'Sit down opposite me, against the wall. On the floor.'

I did as he said.

He was slight and not full grown. Brown hair, dark frightened eyes. Cheeks still round from childhood; the jaw line of an adult. Half boy, half man, with tear stains on his face and his finger on the trigger.

Everything movable in the bare little cabin had been stacked in a neat pile to one side. A heavy table and two solid chairs were the total to be left. No curtains at the single small window. No rugs on the bare wood floor. Two collapsible camp beds, folded and strapped together for transport, leaned against a wall. A pair of skis stood beside them.

No logs by the cold stove, and no visible food.

'It'll be dark soon,' I said. 'Within an hour.'

'I don't care.' He stared at me with burning eyes and unnerving intensity.

'We should go down to Berit's house while we can still see the way.'

'No.'

'We'll freeze up here.'

'I don't care.'

I believed him. Anyone as distracted as he was tended to blot even extreme discomforts out of his mind: and although he had allowed me into the hut he was far from coming down off the high wire. Little tremors of tension ran in his body and twitched his feet. Occasionally the gun shook in his hands. I tried not to think gloomy thoughts.

'We must go,' I said.

'Sit still,' he said fiercely, and the right forefinger curled convulsively. I looked at it. And I sat.

Daylight slowly faded and the cold crept in inexorably. The wind outside whined like a spoilt child, never giving up. I thought I might as well face it: the prospect of the night ahead made the fjord water seem in retrospect as cosy as a heated pool. I put my padded mitts inside my padded pockets and tried to kid myself that my fingers were warm. And it was a minor disaster that the jacket wasn't really long enough for sitting on.

'Mikkel,' I said. 'Just tell me. You'll explode if you don't talk to someone. And I'm here. So just . . . tell me. Whatever you like.'

He stared fixedly through the gathering dusk. I waited a long time.

'I killed him,' he said.

Oh God.

A long pause. Then on a rising note he said it again, 'I killed him.'

'Who?' I said.

Silence.

'How?' I said.

The question surprised him. He took his gaze for one moment off my face and glanced down at the gun.

'I . . . shot . . .'

With an effort I said, 'Did you shoot . . . Arne?'

'Arne . . .' The hysteria rose again. 'No. No. No. Not Arne. I didn't kill Arne. I didn't. I didn't.'

'All right,' I said. 'All right, Mikkel. Let's wait a bit . . . until you can tell me. Until you feel it is the right time to tell me.' I paused. 'Is that OK?'

After a while he said, '*Ja*. OK.'

We waited.

It got darker until it seemed that the only light left was the reflection from the window in his eyes. I could see them long after the rest of him dissolved into one amorphous shadow, two live agonized signals of a mind desperately afraid of the help it desperately needed.

It must have occurred to him as to me that after

total darkness I would be able to jump his gun, because he stirred restlessly on the floor and muttered something in Norwegian, and finally in a much more normal voice said, 'There is a lamp in a box. On top of the things.'

'Shall I find it and light it?'

'*Ja.*'

I stood up stiffly, glad of the chance to move, but sensing him lift the gun to keep me where it mattered.

'I won't try to take the gun away,' I said.

No answer.

The heap of gear was to my right, near the window. I moved carefully, but with many small noises so that he should know where I was and not be alarmed, and felt around for the box on top. Nothing wrong with his memory: the box was there, and the lamp in it, and also a box of matches.

'I've found the lamp,' I said. 'Shall I strike a match?'

A pause.

'*Ja.*'

It proved to be a small gas lamp. I lit it and put it on the table from where it cast a weak white light into every corner. He blinked twice as his irises adjusted, but his concentration never wavered.

'Is there any food?' I asked.

'I'm not hungry.'

'I am.'

'Sit down,' he said. 'Where you were.'

I sat. The gun barrels followed. In the new light I could see down them a lot too well.

Time passed. I lit the lamp at four thirty in the afternoon and it was eight before he began to talk.

By then, if I was anything to go by, he had lost all feeling from the waist down. He wore no gloves and his hands had turned blue-white, but he still held the gun ready, with his finger inside the trigger guard. His eyes still watched. His face, his whole body, were still stiff with near-unbearable tension.

He said suddenly, 'Arne Kristiansen told me that my father was arrested. He told me he was arrested because of you.'

His voice came out high and his breath condensed into a frosty plume.

Once started, he found it easier.

'He said . . . my father wanted us to go to Bergen . . . and on a boat to Stavanger . . . and fly . . .' He stopped.

'And you didn't go,' I said. 'Why didn't you go?'

The gun shook.

'They came in . . .' he said.

I waited.

He said, 'I was talking to him. Outside. About going away.' A pause. 'They came over the hill. On skis, with goggles.' Another pause. 'One of them told Arne to step away from me.' After a longer pause and with an even sharper burst of remembered terror he said, 'He had a knife.'

'Oh Mikkel,' I said.

He talked faster, tumbling it out.

'Arne said, "You can't. You can't. He wouldn't send you to kill his own son. Not Mikkel." He pushed me behind him. He said, "You're crazy. I talked to his father myself. He told me to come here to take Mikkel away." '

He stared across at me with stretched eyes, reliving it.

'They said . . . my father had changed his mind about Arne going. They said they were to take me themselves on a ship to Denmark and wait until my father sent money and instructions. Arne said it was not true. They said . . . it was true . . . and they said . . . Arne was going no further than right here . . . He didn't believe it . . . he said not even my father would do that. He watched only the one with the knife and the other one swung a ski stick and hit him on the head . . . He fell down in the snow . . . I tried to stop them . . . they just pushed me off . . . and they put him on the sleigh . . . they strapped him on . . . and pulled him up the path.'

The panic he had felt then came crowding back into his face. He said painfully, 'I remembered the gun in the cabin . . . I went inside and loaded it . . . and put on my skis and went after them . . . to stop them . . . but when I found them they were coming back . . . without the sleigh . . . and I thought . . . I thought . . . they were going to . . . they were going to . . .'

He took a deep shuddering breath. 'I fired the gun. The one with the knife . . . he fell down . . .'

'I fired again,' he said. 'But the other one was still on his skis . . . So I came back to the cabin because I thought he would come after me . . . I came back to reload the gun. But he didn't come . . . He didn't come . . .

'You came,' he said. 'I thought it was him.'

He stopped.

'Did you know the two men?' I asked. 'Had you ever seen them before?'

'No.'

'How long was it before I came?' I said.

'I don't know. A long time.'

'Hours?'

'I think so.'

I hadn't seen any of them on my way up.

'Killing is wrong,' he said jerkily.

'It depends.'

'No.'

'To defend your life, or someone else's life, it would be all right,' I said.

'I . . . I believe . . . I *know* it is wrong. And yet I . . . when I was so afraid . . .' His high voice cracked. 'I have done it. I despise killing and I've done it. And I would have killed you too. I know I would. If you hadn't jumped.'

'Never mind,' I said; but the horrors were still there in his eyes. Making it deliberately an emotion-reducing question I asked, 'Have you known Arne Kristiansen long?'

'What . . .?' His own voice came down a bit. 'About three years, I suppose.'

'And how well do you know him?'

'Not very well. On the racecourse. That's all.'

'Has your father known him long?'

'I don't think so . . . The same as me. At the races.'

'Are they close friends?'

He said with sudden extreme bitterness, 'My father has no close friends.'

'Will you put the gun down now?' I said.

He looked at it.

'All right.'

He put it beside him on the floor. A relief not to be looking down those two round holes.

The lamp chose that moment to give notice it was running out of gas. Mikkel switched his gaze from me to the table, but the message of fading light didn't seem to pierce through the inner turmoil.

'The lamp is going out,' I said. 'Is there a spare gas cylinder?'

He slowly shook his head.

'Mikkel,' I said. 'It is freezing and it will soon be dark. If we are to survive the night we must keep warm.'

No response.

'Are you listening?'

'What?'

'You are going to have to face life as it is.'

'I . . . can't . . .'

'Are there any blankets?'

'There is one.'

I began to try to stand up and he reached immediately for the gun.

'Don't be silly,' I said. 'I won't hurt you. And you won't shoot me. So let's just both relax, huh?'

He said uncertainly. 'You had my father arrested.'

'Do you know why?'

'Not . . . not really.'

I told him about the oil transaction, playing down the disloyalty, to put it no higher, that Per Bjørn had shown to his country, but there was, it seemed, nothing basically wrong with Mikkel's brains. He was silent for some time after I'd finished and the muscles slowly relaxed limb by limb.

'Once he had been found out,' he said, 'he would lose his job. He would lose the respect of everyone. He wouldn't be able to live like that . . . not my father.'

His voice at last was sane and controlled; and almost too late. The lamp was going out.

'The blanket,' he said, 'is in the beds.'

He tried to stand up and found his legs were as numb and useless as mine, if not more so. It kicked him straight back to practical sense.

'I'm cold!'

'So am I.'

He looked across, seeing our predicament squarely for the first time.

'Stand up,' he said. 'Walk about.'

Easier said, but it had to be done.

'Can we light the stove?' I said. 'There are four more matches, the cardboard boxes, and the table and chairs, if we can break them up.'

We had both by then tottered to our feet. The lamp shone with one candle power, sadly.

'There is no axe,' Mikkel said.

The lamp went out.

'I'm sorry,' he said.

'Never mind.'

We jumped up and down in total darkness. Funny if it hadn't been urgent. Blood started circulating again, though, to the places where it was needed, and after half an hour or so we were both warm enough to give it a rest.

'I can find the blanket,' Mikkel said, and did so. 'Shall we share it?'

'We certainly shall.'

We both wore warm jackets and he, when he remembered where he'd put them, had a cap and mitts like my own. We laid the folded canvas beds on an insulating foundation of cardboard boxes, and wrapped ourselves from the waist down in one cocoon in the single blanket, sitting close together to share every scrap of warmth. It was too dark to see what he was thinking, but there were faint tremors still, occasionally, through his body.

'I took the rest of the bedding down to Berit's house yesterday,' he said. 'On the sleigh.'

'Pity.'

The word switched his thoughts. He said abruptly, 'Do you think Arne is dead?'

'I don't know,' I said. But I did think so.

'What will happen to me, for killing that man?'

'Nothing. Just tell it as you told me. No one will blame you.'

'Are you sure?'

'Yes.'

'I am as bad as anyone else who kills,' he said, but this time there was adult acceptance and despair in his voice, not hysteria. I wondered if it were possible for a boy to age ten years in one night, because it would be better for him if he could.

'Tell me about Bob Sherman,' I said; and felt the jolt that went through him at the name.

'I . . . can't . . .'

'Mikkel . . . I know that Bob brought the stolen surveys from England to give to your father . . .'

'No,' he interrupted.

'What, then?'

'He had to deliver them to Arne. I didn't know they were for my father when I . . .' He stopped dead.

'When you what?'

'I mustn't tell you. I can't.'

In the darkness I said calmly, almost sleepily, 'Did Bob tell you he had brought a package?'

He said unwillingly, 'Yes.'

I yawned. 'When?'

283

'When I met him in Oslo. The night he came.'

I wondered if he felt in his turn the thud with which that news hit me.

'Where in Oslo?' I said casually.

'He was outside the Grand with his saddle and his overnight bag. I was walking home from a friend's house, and I stopped. He said he might go and catch the tram. I asked him if he would like some coffee first, so we walked along to our house. I carried his saddle.' He paused. 'I liked Bob. We were friends.'

'I know,' I said.

'My father was out. He usually is. Mother was watching television. Bob and I went into the kitchen, and I made the coffee. We ate some cake my mother had made.'

'What did you talk about?'

'At first about the horses he was riding the next day ... Then he said he had brought a package from England, and he'd opened it, and it didn't contain what he'd been told. He said he had to give it to Arne Kristiansen at the races but he was going to ask for a bit more money before he handed it over.'

His body trembled against mine within the blanket.

'He was laughing about it, really. He said they'd told him it was pornography, but it wasn't, and he didn't know what it was even though he'd seen it. Then he took the package out of his case and told me to look.'

He stopped.

'And,' I said, 'when you saw what was in the package, you knew what it was?'

'I'd seen papers like that before . . . I mean . . . I knew it was an oil survey. Yes.'

'Did you tell Bob what it was?'

'Yes. I did. We talked about it a bit.'

'And then?'

'It was late. Too late for the tram. Bob took a taxi out to Gunnar Holth's stable, and I went to bed.'

'What happened the next day?'

'I promised . . . I promised I wouldn't tell anybody. I didn't tell the police. I mustn't tell you. Especially not you. I know that.'

'All right,' I said.

Time passed. It was almost too cold to think.

'I told my father about Bob Sherman's package on the way to the races,' he said. 'He took me in the car. I only told him for something to say. Because I thought he might be interested. But he didn't say much. He never does. I never know what he's thinking.'

'Nor do I,' I said.

'I have heard people say he looks kindest when he is being most cruel. When I was small, I heard it first.'

'Is he cruel to you?'

'No. Just . . . cold. But he is my father.'

'Yes.'

'I think I want to tell you . . . but I can't.'

'All right.'

A long time passed. His breath and body movements

betrayed his wakefulness and the churning thoughts in his mind.

'Mr Cleveland? Are you awake?'

'David,' I said.

'David . . . Do you think he meant those men to kill me?'

'No, I don't.'

'He told them where to come. He told me to come to Finse. He told Arne Kristiansen to come to Finse. And those men.'

'He did,' I said. 'But I should think they spoke the truth. I should think he meant them to take you out of the country, after they had dealt with Arne. I should think they were very clumsy to let you see them actually attack Arne, but then they have more strength than brains, those two. Arne is the only one who could go into court and give conclusive evidence against your father, and I do think that your father is ruthless enough to have him killed to prevent that.'

'Why . . . why do you think so?'

'Because he sent those two men after me, too.'

I told him about the boat in the fjord, the knife in Chelsea, the bomb in Erik's car.

'They're terrible men,' he said. 'They frightened me the instant I saw them.'

He relapsed into silence. I could almost feel him thinking, suffering, working it all out.

'David?'

'Yes?'

'It was my fault Bob died.'

'Certainly not.'

'But if I hadn't told my father that Bob knew he'd brought an oil survey . . .'

'Arne would have told him,' I said flatly. 'You can go on saying if for ever. If Bob hadn't opened the package. If your father hadn't been ruthless enough to get rid of him. But all these things happened. They all happened because your father is both greedy and proud, which is always a pretty deadly combination. But also he learned how to live a secret life when he was young. Against the Nazis, it was good. Everyone admired him. I should think he's never lost the feeling that anything anti-authority is daring and therefore all right. I should think he put the police into the place of the Nazis, as the enemy to be outwitted. He thinks like lightning, he gives away nothing under questioning, he coolly takes tremendous risks, he arranges without mercy for people to die. He's still acting the way he did when he was twenty. He always will.'

Time passed.

'David . . .'

'Yes?'

'I'll have to tell you,' he said.

I took a deep breath. It felt icy in my lungs.

'Go on,' I said.

He paused again. Then he said, 'I was talking to Bob at the races. He laughed and told me it was all fixed,

Arne was going to drive him to the airport afterwards and pay him extra for the package.'

He stopped.

I waited.

His voice went on, hesitant but at last committed.

'By the end of the races it was dark. I went out to the car to wait for my father. He is often late because of being on the committee. I sat in the car and waited for him. I hadn't talked to him at all at the races. I usually don't see him much there. He's always busy.'

He stopped again. His breathing grew heavier, more disturbed.

'Most of the cars went. Then two people came past and in some passing headlights I saw they were Bob and Arne. I was going to call out to them . . . I wish I had . . . but I couldn't get the window down fast enough . . . and then they were over by Arne's car. They were talking face to face. I could only see them now and then, you see, when car lights pointed that way as people went home. But I saw another man walk up behind Bob and raise his arm. He held something shiny . . . Then he brought it down . . .'

He stopped. Gulped a bit. Went on. 'The next time I could see, there were only two people there. I thought . . . I couldn't *believe* . . . And then one of them turned and came towards our car. I was scared . . .'

He shuddered violently.

'But he just opened the boot and threw into it something which clinked, and then he got into the driving seat, and he was smiling.'

A long pause.

'Then he saw me sitting there, and he looked absolutely astonished. And he said . . . he said . . . "Mikkel! I'd forgotten you were at the races." '

His voice was full of pain.

'He'd forgotten me. Forgotten me.'

He was trying not to cry.

'My father,' he said. 'My father killed Bob Sherman.'

CHAPTER EIGHTEEN

We went down to Finse at first light, him sliding easily on his skis, me scrunching and slipping in my city shoes. If I looked anything like he did I had blue grey circles round my eyes, hollows at the corners of my mouth, and a certain overall air of extreme weariness.

He had said little more during the night. He had rolled his head on to my shoulder at one point and fallen exhaustedly asleep, and in the early morning, when he stirred, he had been calm and apparently untroubled, as if the final unburdening of the horror he'd lived with through eight long weeks had set him quietly free.

I left him with the warm comforting people of Finse, and went up the mountain again with several local men. This time I went on skis, shuffling along inexpertly up the slope. They waited for me, making jokes. They had cheerful faces, carefree smiles. And the sun came wanly through the clouds, the first time I'd seen it in Norway.

We reached the hut and went on past it, up beyond where the path petered out into a flat field of snow.

Two of the men were pulling a sleigh, a lightweight affair sliding easily on ski-like runners; just like the one old Berit has, they said.

Brown eyes was lying face down in the snow.

Dead.

But he hadn't died from gunshot wounds: or not primarily. He'd died from exposure and cold.

The men from Finse looked in silence at the trail leading away behind his body. He'd been pulling himself along, crawling. The snow where he'd been was streaked black with his blood.

They wrapped him in canvas, put him on the sleigh, and turned to go to Finse.

'I'll go that way,' I said, pointing to where brown eyes had come from.

They nodded, consulted, and sent a man with me, as they didn't trust my rudimentary ability on skis.

We followed the blood-stained trail up a shallow slope and on to a sort of plateau whose far edge was a smooth horizon against a pale grey sky. The trail ended in a jumble of tracks which the man from Finse rapidly interpreted.

'This is where he was shot. See the blood. There was another man with him.' He pointed to a set of ski marks setting off at a tangent across virgin snow. 'That man is an expert cross-country skier. He went fast. He left the other man lying wounded in the snow. He did not come back with help. If he had, he could have followed the trail of blood.'

Yellow eyes had just upped and left. But Knut would find him in the end.

'The two men came across to here skiing fast and easily,' my guide said, and pointed to tracks stretching away across the plateau.

'There are other tracks over there,' he said, turning to his right and stretching out a well gloved hand.

'Let's look,' I said.

We went over.

'Two men,' he said, 'pulling a loaded sleigh.'

Although I expected it, it hit in my gut.

'They came that way,' I said, pointing back towards the hut.

He nodded. We went back along the trail until we found the marks of Mikkel's skis beside it.

'The boy came to here. Stopped. Then he turned and went back. You can see from his tracks that he was disturbed when he came. And panic stricken when he left. Look at the depth and the sharpness and the small steps.'

'We might find the cartridges,' I said.

He nodded. We looked for a while and found both of them, bright orange cylinders on the snow.

'And now . . .' I gestured ahead along the trail which Mikkel had been following: two men and a loaded sleigh.

The marks ran regularly across the plateau towards the horizon. We followed.

The horizon proved to be not the end of the world,

but the brow of a hill. Down the other side the slope was steep, short, and sharp edged, and far beyond it, mile upon mile, lay a vista of snow-scattered peaks. We were standing at the top of the cliffs above the lake where Berit lived.

The marks of the two men on skis stopped at the brow of the hill, and turned back.

The sleigh marks ran on straight and true to the edge.

'I want to go down there,' I said, and unclipped my skis.

My guide didn't like it, but produced a rope from round his waist. He tied me to it, and paid it out foot by foot, standing four square and solid at the top of the slope.

I went down slowly in my borrowed boots, finding the snow surprisingly glassy and having to be careful not to slide. Having to concentrate, too, on not feeling giddy, and finding it as difficult as ever. When I stood at length on the edge I could see all the lake stretching away, with Berit's house a crimson blob far down to the left.

Beside my feet the marks of the runners looked shallow and crisp, speaking of speed. And they ran on without pity, pointing straight out into space.

The drop in front was six hundred feet, perpendicular. The ruffled green water lay secretively below. Nothing else. Nothing to see.

Arne, I thought. Flying through the air on a sleigh, down to his death.

Arne . . . who didn't look over his shoulder the one time the enemy was really there.

Arne, my treacherous friend.

You would have sworn that round the snowy cliffs you could hear crashing chords of Beethoven echoing in the wind.

extracts reading groups
competitions books new
discounts extracts extracts
competitions
books
new
events books
extracts new titles reading groups
interviews
events extracts
discounts
new books events
events new
discounts extracts discounts
www.panmacmillan.com
extracts events reading groups
competitions books extracts new
reading groups
events
reading groups
books